JUST THE STORY OF

"TWO WINGS"

A Lakota Plains Indian

Valerie A. Lancaster

Dedicated to my

North American Indian Friends

in this world . . .

and the next

Story and Verse

from

"Just Poems"

Beaten Track

First published 2015 by Beaten Track Publishing
Copyright © 1992, 2015 Valerie A. Lancaster

A CIP catalogue record for this book
is available from the British Library.

ISBN: 978 1 910635 14 8

Beaten Track Publishing,
Burscough. Lancashire.
www.beatentrackpublishing.com

Foreword

>>>> By the Author <<<<

I have admired the North American Indian ever since my childhood and as I have grown, my love for them has increased. This book has been written with the deepest respect.

The story of "Two Wings" is fictional, but in Chapter Eleven the account of the Sun Dance is drawn from personal memories, for my husband and I were greatly honoured to be invited by a Lakota friend to be his guests, when he danced for his ninth year.

Our presence there is an experience I treasure deeply and will never forget, for the love generated throughout the four days, was incredible.

These Sacred Ceremonies are not open to the public and he had to ask permission from his Medicine Man, for us to attend. I in turn have now asked our North American Indian friend if I may include this Sacred Rite in my book. His reply was 'Yes' . . . saying he knew I would portray it in an honest and respectful way – and this I have done.

Many times my thoughts drift back to the Badlands of South Dakota and to the Lakota people whom I continue to admire and love. Thanks to their friendship, in my mind I can enjoy again and again – the spiritual beauty and healing power of their Sacred Sun Dance.

The Plains Indians, especially the Lakota, or Sioux as the Whiteman called them, were the most spiritual of all the North American Tribes . . . and their teachings can still be heard today.

Valerie A. Lancaster

Chapter	CONTENTS	Page

CONTENTS

CHAPTER ONE

Our Village and its People

Situated at Long Grass Creek in the curve of a meandering river, our village is flanked by the water on one side and the forest on the other. Most of our tipis are in this area but the lodges of the Elders are where the river divides into two for a short way, its waters almost surrounding them. Our Medicine Man has his lodge amongst a small group of Silver Birch trees, looking out to the mountains beyond. Here the younger children like to play and their mothers feel happy, knowing they are safe. To the south is the forest which stretches for many miles and to the west, the vast prairie where the great buffalo herds roam. It is there we can view the distant storms with their long jagged flashes of lightning cutting across the sky and lighting up the horizon. We hear the thunder roll over the lowlands and echo loudly through the mountains to the north. These mountains are the Black Hills and they are sacred to our people. Looking out to the Great Plains we can see the swaying grasslands dancing in the wind, as if waving to the sky.

The part of the river flowing past our village is not too wide and has small streams running into it from the woodland. Our ponies graze between two of these streams which they seem to accept as natural boundaries. We are able to leave them there untethered, to wander around quite content. They are handsome looking animals, their smooth coats showing different coloured patches of white, browns and fawn. They have a well-defined head with clear bright eyes that hold an expression of loyalty and trust, mixed in with a rugged independence and they are swift and agile with slender legs and long tails. Just like our dogs, our ponies are very good at bringing our attention to anything which is unusual or threatening, for they are extremely alert, being quick to respond to danger.

The dogs are also adept at guarding our children, as well as being their playful companions. They are truly faithful, for living close to the forest means there have been a number of occasions when the great bear has appeared and the dogs are usually the first to try and chase him away. What a magnificent beast the Grizzly Bear is – and how we admire his courage and greatness. Only if he becomes a constant threat, do we feel right in tracking him down. We send out special prayers to encourage him to stay away, but sometimes his visits continue and we realise that maybe, the time has come for his spirit to journey home. Then sadly, we are forced to do what is necessary for the safety of all, yet we continue to honour him and wear his coat with pride. Both he and Tatanka the mighty buffalo, are a symbol of strength and power and we consider ourselves privileged to walk in their domain and witness their presence. When we hunt Tatanka, it is to feed and clothe our people and only the weak and injured are taken. Every part of his huge body is used, for it would be as an insult to him if anything were wasted. Before we take his life, loving thoughts are always sent out to him. We ask the Great Spirit to help Tatanka travel safely across to the Spirit Land, where he can once again roam forever free, grazing upon windswept grasses beneath far-reaching skies, in those wide open spaces we have seen within our dreams.

My constant companion is the Hawk whom I found as a young fledgling born early one spring, when the snow still covered the ground and the soil lay hard and bare. He was weak and lost . . . and made me his friend. I have loved him ever since. He is a free spirit, born to soar in the air above and my own spirit rises up with his, whenever he moves across the sky or skims over the flowing waters. How I envy him as he rides those high thermals and my heart beats so fast when he swoops downwards again, to level out and fly swiftly along just above the valley floor. I then watch him circling around before veering upwards into the trees, never once faltering on his set course. When I walk through the forest, he is my eyes and out on the prairie and in the tall grass, he lets nothing take me by surprise.

We like to rest, he and I, on the banks of the river until he glides gracefully down to the water's edge, where he flaps his wings excitedly, as I plunge into the coolness of the deep pools. This river originates in the Black Hills, with their pointed peaks and deep gullies and brings with it, not only the fresh water from the mountain streams, but also the memories of our forefathers. These mountains are a place of great beauty, a place befitting to hold their mortal remains. When possible, we make long journeys into their foothills where we stay and meditate, before continuing up into their loftier heights. Whilst there, we feel the peaceful presence of our passed loved ones, blending with the natural elements found all around. We are at one with ourselves and each other, knowing how our Ancestors are close and that they enjoy us being where their own memories lie, for when on Earth, they themselves would spend time amongst these wild and rugged peaks.

We stay for many days, taking in the immense freedom and exhilaration that is experienced in such splendid surroundings. Standing quietly on the edge of the great precipices, we view the land stretching out before us, with the never-ending plains and prairie and the lush green of the wide valleys and woodlands. The rich grasslands provide the hay which feeds our animals throughout the long bleak winter days, as well as keeping both them and our people warm. From this great height we can also see the blue of the river leading to our own village, which nestles in one of its many bends and is partly hidden by the trees at the edge of the forest. During the long hard winter months these trees offer much needed protection from the bitterly cold winds and the forest gives us wood for our campfires. It shields our ponies and helps the surrounding wildlife to survive.

The winding river is the life-blood of our village and we are ever thankful for its constant flow, for although its many streams may freeze, the river continues to run and quench our thirst, no matter how deep the snow may lie. It waters the land when the rains are gone and carries us safely to distant parts. It both refreshes and uplifts us, for along it can be found small waterfalls and hidden coves, where it is good to pause and relax – or maybe just sit and dream. The river's flow is the pulse of our everyday life. Many animals and birds enjoy its cooling balm and drink gratefully from it . . . and from its small creeks. Upon the fertile banks grow different kinds of herbs, flowers, berries and grasses. Fish swim in this river but the larger fish tend to be in the deeper waters, further south. There, the ground is more barren and has large open stretches of much calmer water.

To the west are the rapids and it is on them the young men of our village delight in testing their skills. They ride the churning, white-topped waves in their strong and carefully made canoes and even the daughters of our Tribe are quite taken with the thrill and excitement of the many challenges set. They appear in little groups, as if from nowhere, shyly talking together as they watch the battle between the fast swirling waters and the young men, who are desperately trying to manoeuvre their canoes through the boulders and rocks, eager to show how courageous and energetic they are. I am one of these young men . . . and I too am anxious to impress those who are now cheering us on. My friends and I are fairly well matched with each other – but not with the forces of nature. More often than not, our adventure ends with us clinging to our overturned canoes, quite convinced that on the next attempt we will do better. Maybe one day we will, but for the moment we are winning not the battle to stay afloat, but the more important battle for knowledge. This time we are learning respect for the immense power of Mother Nature.

Although I am just like the rest of the sons in our village, I am maybe not quite as impulsive as most of my friends. The reason is that I tend to balance the thoughts in my head with the words heard from deep within, for I enjoy the company of those whom I know walk here unseen, from times long ago. They talk to me often and in various ways ... by the touch of the breeze or the rustling of leaves, through the soft murmuring stream or the gushing waterfall, in the cry of a bird or the howl of the wolf. They may come on the scent of a flower or on the wings of a moth and I know they are all a part of me – and that I am a part of them. As a youth, I have not yet found my position within our community, but that will be decided upon soon enough. Like my parents, I am tall and slim and have brown eyes and bronzed skin. My hair is dark and worn loose around my shoulders, although sometimes I braid it into one long plait, which then falls down the centre of my back.

My father is the eldest son of our Medicine Man and I hope that one day I will be able to walk in my grandfather's footsteps and share in his learning. My ambition is to follow his healing ways and to inherit his understanding and love for all things ... but only time will tell. At the moment I am relishing the life of a young North American Lakota Indian from the Oglala Band of the Great Sioux Nation, living on the edge of the Plains, with the sky above me and the richness of the red earth beneath my feet. I have the sun to guide me in the day and the moon and stars to follow during the night. The moon holds a special significance for all our people. Its penetrating light reaches out through the darkness, its beams forming a pathway for our eyes to follow . . . a path leading up to the vastness of the Universe. It takes us to a place far beyond the view of our worldly sight and far beyond the understanding of men, yet to ponder on it stretches our thoughts and helps each one to look deeper into the hidden beauty which lies above, as well as around us. The twinkling stars shining so brightly, are like the tiny fireflies glowing in the quiet of night, reflecting the silver glow of the moon itself.

This far-off moon fills us full of wonder. Sitting in the coolness of its shadow, we now hear the haunting cry of the wolf as he sings with the rest of his kind – a song which seems to match the mystery and magic of the moonlight all around. When the air is crisp, it is as though each note is magnified a hundred times, each varying tone echoing across the open prairie. This sound is truly haunting . . . but so very beautiful to hear. It is a jubilant sound, a sound of freedom, for the wolf travels freely with his pack and knows each secret trail, each hidden track. He is like a phantom that comes alive with the fall of night, moving with such stealth and ease. He troubles us not and rarely comes too near. We admire him, for he is a noble creature with the pale blue eyes of a clear mountain stream. As we quietly watch, he and his young family romp joyfully along the banks of the river. They are out on their nightly prowl and have just moved down to the waters edge, to drink from one of the many small pools which lie trapped in the rocks nearby. Even though we are in the season of the sun, their coats are thick and long.

Together with the alpha pair and their pups are four adolescent males, three young females and two older females, who are now becoming tired of exploring this part of the river and are preparing to leave. We silently watch as they turn and retreat, quite certain our presence has not gone unnoticed by the older and wiser members of the pack. They seem to accept we show no malice towards them and that we are content to simply share a few brief moments of their nightly trek. When we adorn ourselves with the coat of our brother the wolf, it is because he has recently left this World ... to continue his wanderings in that land beyond our sphere. On rare occasions, as happens with the great bear, a lone individual may stalk our village and then we again have to do what we must, but it is done with respect and love. We admire all creatures – it is our way, for it is the way of the Great Spirit. We know all things are joined by his infinite love for each and everyone. We know the wolf is a part of our natural family and shares this beautiful land with us. We feel proud to wear the earthly coat which he leaves here, knowing how his spirit is once more free and happy to roam much further afield.

I can understand the wolf's love of this rugged landscape and often wonder if our dogs ever feel tempted to join their wild cousins, out on the distant plains ... to run with them through the tall grasses and play amongst the foothills of the majestic mountains. Perhaps though, their own inner-self warns them that – outside our camp, they would have to compete for their food, after maybe hunting for many days. Do they sense the security in the care and companionship given to them here and would they miss the chatter and almost constant attention of at least one child? As I think on these things, I wonder if we are guilty of taking away some of their basic instincts, but they are hardly ever restricted and seem happy to return our friendship.

The night is still and the stars in the sky glow brighter as the moon continues to rise, before starting to fade once more from our view. The cycle of life is forever moving onwards – until it arrives back at where it began. Our Sacred Hoop enfolds our people in an eternal bond. Everything within its circle is connected and every tiny thing is a part of the whole, for we are all woven into Mother Nature's colourful patchwork of life.

The threads of time draw us slowly forward, from springtime to springtime, from today's sunrise to the following sunrise, from one moment to the next . . . as we grow, experience and learn. Since our arrival from the Spirit Land to our return – we journey on. Truly, the circle is never ending. Our body in old age is as frail as it was when it took that first breath as a tiny new babe, yet our spirit will hopefully be strengthened and enriched with the different lessons it has gained.

I quietly think on these things as we retire to our tipis, to find that magical sleep state which not only refreshes our body, but allows our spirit to join again with those loved ones who have indeed, moved ahead. Perhaps tonight, I will wander through the stars in the heavens above or maybe I will journey with the wolf, enjoying the special freedom that slumber brings. It is not long before I fall into a deep sleep, as the night draws its veil of mystery over those who succumb to its peaceful state, for thoughts now fade . . . as sweet oblivion conquers all.

I am a child of the Universe, no more and no less than my spirit unfolds. I was once the future and will one day be the past, but at the moment I am part of the present, here in this body which represents me. I have learnt many things in my childhood and met with many people, but ahead stretches the most interesting challenge of all – the challenge of becoming a man. My spirit may have known many lifetimes which are now hidden from view, but it is in this present state that I can further enrich its light and thus increase its love.

So now I dream . . . not of the stars, nor of the wolf, but of those mountains to the north where I am ever eager to go. Beyond the mist I see their peaks reaching up to the sky and sense the power and strength held therein. Breathing in the clear air, I enjoy the breezes caressing my face as I listen to the wind whistling along the gullies far below. I am fully aware of the energies flowing in the ground beneath my feet and of the healing being given from the trees. My Hawk is with me and he circles slowly upwards, drawing my spirit ever higher, allowing me to look down on the splendour wrapped all around, as the colours of dawn start to gradually show.

>>>> <<<<

"Just the Spirit of the North American Indian"

Of all the different kinds of men who've walked
upon this Earth, it was the humble Indian who knew
that from his birth - he was of the Great Spirit, part of
nature as a whole, yes, spirit with a body
. . . a person with a soul.

The North American Indian understood
the Spirit Laws, his mother was the Earthplane, his life
was but a pause, as he travelled on his journey passing through
the many spheres, growing thus in knowledge -
knowing happiness and tears.

He recognised this earthly life was given
as a gift . . . to forward his progression, his mind
and soul uplift, facing up to problems which he knew would
help him learn, gaining strength and wisdom
to pass on in his turn.

With arms outstretched to greet the dawn
and face raised to the sun, he chanted his own words to
God and bade the day 'Welcome'. He thanked him for the beauty
of his beloved plains, the mountains with their ruggedness,
the forests with their rains.

Because his life was simple he related to
each thing, he ran amongst the creatures, soared with
eagles on the wing, he came to know their movements and read
their every thought, he treated them as brothers
- and in return was taught.

Taught to blend with nature, attune to
spirit friends, seek advice from Elders who proved
life never ends, learn about the flowers, the bushes and
the trees, using bark and roots and herbs,
to chase away disease.

Many were great mediums and healing
power had found, they knew well of the Spirit World –
their 'happy hunting ground'. They had no fear of dying and
only wished to be . . . in harmony with all things,
with honour living free.

Free to roam the vast prairie, its beauty
their delight, to feel the wind and taste the rain and
see the stars at night, foregoing worldly goods for those of
spirit and the land, keeping few possessions for
all nature was at hand.

They only hunted buffalo for meat and
skins to wear, they still loved and respected him and
offered up a prayer - to guide him to the Spirit World where
he would live again . . . the hearts were kind and gentle,
of these strong and fearless men.

At sunrise and at sunset he worshipped
on his own, face to face with nature and the God he'd
always known would always walk beside him and all his troubles
share, he had no shrine or temple
- for God was everywhere.

Because they were so spiritual their
Ancestors return, to guide those in the Earth Sphere
who really seek to learn and further spirit teachings, telling
how life carries on, love binding all together . . .
the Great Spirit in each one.

28.9.93

"Just the Freedom of the Wolf"

Out from the woodland when the air is still
and the sun drops slowly behind each hill,
quiet shadows can be seen
- venturing towards the stream.
There in the moonlight's gentle glow
sleek silhouettes begin to show
and inquisitive faces now appear,
making sure each way is clear
before they let the pups draw near.

Stealthy footsteps pave the way,
then younger ones, leap and play
upon the mossy riverbank,
yet all are conscious of their rank
. . . following the alpha pair
who hold the pack within their care.
Though faithful to their lifelong mate,
both to one and all relate -
and thus the family's strength stays great.

They lap the water clear and cool
from a nearby rocky pool,
the she-wolf resting on a mound
. . . her offspring chasing siblings round.
The male now leaves the river's edge
to stand alone upon a ledge
where he sniffs the fresh night air,
his senses roused, fully aware.
The others pause - this moment to share.

On lifting his head towards the moon
there comes from him a haunting tune,
a powerful sound which travels far . . .
caressing the heavens from star to star,
across the plains, through valleys wide,
along canyons steep and mountainside.
The pack joins in 'til eventually
the prairie resounds with a symphony
- that echoes the joys of living free.

12.2.13

12

CHAPTER TWO

Life in our Village

Our village is a haven where we can enjoy the beauty of Mother Earth and where our children learn about the many wonders of the life which flourishes all around them, from the features of the land itself to the various creatures with whom we share this world. Most significant are the buffalo who traverse the Great Plains and wide open valleys. Without them we could not survive. We know when our people first came to live on the Earth they found it to be a world of beauty, but they took what they saw for granted. Then winter arrived and they became very cold and wet... and extremely hungry. They cried out to the Great Spirit, who took pity on them – and sent the mighty buffalo to clothe and feed them all. We both admire and honour this magnificent beast. Grazing amongst the buffalo are white-tailed deer and pronghorn antelope, watched by the inquisitive and amusing prairie dogs, whose homes are hidden under the ground. Wolves and coyote roam the prairie and woodlands, while tall majestic moose wade in lakes and rivers and mule deer and elk wander through the forests.

As well as these, there are the many smaller animals. They include beaver, porcupine, skunk, river otter, honey badger, red fox, muskrat, squirrels, tiny chipmunks and a host of others. We are also mindful of black bears and grizzlies and of the elusive bobcat, lynx and cougar. Often we come across the discarded skin of a snake or hear his distinctive hiss or warning rattle, before actually noticing him in the longer grass. On some occasions we see him sunbathing amongst the rocks. Above us fly buzzards and eagles from the high peaked mountains, while red-tailed hawks, prairie falcons and other birds of prey can also be seen, soaring in ever-rising circles. We enjoy the sound of the songbirds and woodpecker and frequently catch sight of the beautiful bluebird. Our homeland has a great richness of wildlife and we are taught to understand and appreciate all these different species and to treat them as brothers. The landscape itself changes ... from woodlands and forests to green prairie and grasslands, from far-reaching plains to wide valleys and tall jagged mountains, from small isolated buttes to deep canyons and winding rivers. Each of these varied features holds a special interest in our heart.

As young children, we learned about the sun and moon and of the stars in the heavens above. We became familiar with the rocks and stones, shrubs and trees, as well as the tracks of the creatures who walk, often unseen, beside and around us. Each child is taught the songs of the various birds and understands the cry of the wolf. They quickly start to recognise the bark of the deer and the deep growl of a bear. They respond to the touch of the breeze and to the call of the wild, enjoying their new found awareness and the sense of added freedom it brings. They listen to the croaking of the frogs at night-time and the chirping of the crickets in the day and they marvel at the skill seen in the building of the bird's nest and the beaver's dam. As with children everywhere, the young of our village are very precious to us. They are our future as well as the reminder of our past and eventually they will become the bearers of more children ... and of further generations. The girls of our Tribe help their mothers to gather plants and herbs, flowers and berries, roots and bark and are shown how to prepare and cook the foods that sustain us. They learn to clean and tan different animal hides and are also taught how to make and sew our garments. They sit happily together, the younger girls busy threading coloured beads into strands, before plaiting them into hair and anklet bands. It is our women who are responsible for the making and erecting of our tipis, which are round like the nest of a bird. The older women enjoy weaving colourful shawls depicting scenes of adventures known, while our elderly men tell exciting stories of brave deeds done ... and of even braver men. They talk about distant places and of strange customs, but best of all is when they speak about the great buffalo herds and the sacred mountains found in the north.

One of the most important members of the village is my own grandfather, our Medicine Man. There are special parts of the woodland to which he alone ventures. This is where he talks with the Nature Spirits, to further develop his knowledge and healing skills. He knows the forest well and is fully aware of those places from which he can replenish his healing balms and potions. Amongst the trees he also finds the solace and strength he needs to renew both his physical and spiritual energies. He speaks to the four winds and can, at times, summon the rain. He pays homage to the sun, greeting it every morning as it brings the daylight and standing before it in the evening, as it slowly descends. He relates to the moon and stars and he understands the passing of time and the birth of the four seasons. He senses the changes in the air, enabling him to keep in touch with the movements of the animals and birds. My grandfather is both a trusted friend and advisor to one and all – from the difficult child to the sensitive youth, from the confused young mother, to the dying old man. He sees many things and has many visions. He is a great healer and knows well of his people's desires, for he can read their innermost thoughts and so shares in both their joy and their pain.

The lodge of our Medicine Man stands slightly apart from the others and is surrounded by trees. It always seems to evoke an air of mystery and though the day may be clear and bright, there sometimes appears to be a shimmering mist drifting around and about it. Smoke has been seen to rise from the top, even when there is no fire burning inside. It stands no taller and indeed is no larger than the other tipis, but it does have more markings upon it. Within are many articles relating to his healing and mystic powers. They are tied in neat clusters and their shapes and colours are quite fascinating to me. As soon as you enter this lodge you are aware of a welcoming presence. It radiates not just from him and his beloved wife, but from the spirits of those who work with him. They come from the great World of Spirit, a place that lies beyond our earthly eyes but exists all around and which at times, can intermingle with this world, depending on the conditions and degrees of love that are present.

Often grandfather steps over into this other world, for it is as he says – so very near. To journey there is not to know distance as we know it here, but to simply move from this dimension into the dimensions of spirit. It is but a step away, not the step taken by any normal means but by a movement of the mind, motivated through sincere thought. To enter this other place we need to adjust our physical vibrations to match those of our spirit within. All life pulsates on varying frequencies and to tune into these frequencies is to journey through time and through space. The ways of the Spirit are quite simple, but it is this simplicity that seems to confuse the minds of men. Nature's own laws are simple – only man complicates them. The creatures of the wild accept and follow their reasoning, they do not try to alter and manipulate the ways of the Great Spirit. How very wise they are … and how close to their own spirit-selves do they exist.

I love to enter my grandfather's tipi, this tipi which is so full of love, friendship and understanding and spend time sitting therein. I enjoy the tantalising aroma that swirls in the air – the mixture of herbs and flowers from the wild, together with the freshness of the pine. Most of all, I love the smell of wood and aromatic smoke, even though the fire is unlit and the burnt embers are cold. It reminds me of times spent sitting around the large campfires, which are specially built when the Elders summon all the menfolk to join with them in talk and in song. Sometimes we sit and listen only to the beat of the drum, for the drum speaks the language of the Redman. It stirs something deep inside him, renewing his love of this wilderness to which he belongs. Its hypnotic tone frees his spirit and awakens his heart and invites him to join in the rhythm of its beat. The sound of the drum travels loudly through our village, spreading out across the prairie, out towards the Black Hills and the resting place of our forefathers. Those who are listening carefully, hear the answers sent back. Some may tend to think they are merely an echo . . . but we of our kind know this is not so. On other occasions we listen only to the crackling of the wood on the fire and concentrate on the sparks floating upwards with the rising smoke. Often while doing this, the Elders speak out through visions received and our Medicine Man dances around within the circle, appearing to blend with his own movements into the shape of the flames dancing in the centre of the fire. What a joining of energies takes place on these spiritual evenings spent around our Circles of Light. What feelings are known, what joys savoured, what interests shared . . . for here is a meeting of like-minded souls.

These thoughts are with me now as I sit in the dimly lit lodge of my grandfather. I am completely relaxed with my legs folded and my hands resting on each knee. My back is straight, my head held level with eyes closed. I have always been so happy and contented here and even the occasional murmurings of my grandmother could never distract me from my peaceful thinking. My thoughts quietly drift and awaken memories of times which lie hidden deep inside my inner being. My spirit again rejoices in the warmth of the love wrapped around me, enfolding me in its blissful balm. I am able to move away from the reality of this life, to a far, far greater reality, encompassing the natural existence of life eternal. Entering a consciousness filled with swirls of living colour, gentle touches and unspoken words complete the full awareness of my oneness with life itself. Eventually I arise and feeling quite elated, join my grandmother for a cooling drink, which not only quenches my thirst but also helps to clear my thoughts and so re-adjust my mind.

My grandmother is a kindly soul and her face is open and truthful, with sparkling eyes that speak of a great tenderness and love. She is the kind of person with whom you can feel completely at ease and in whose company you can be yourself. She has such an atmosphere of harmony around her that wherever she goes, people feel happy to return her smile. I can remember standing at her knee as a toddler and being cradled by her, when just a tiny babe. She seems to be there whenever anyone or anything needs support or reassurance. I know she will always be there for me. I love her dearly and always will. My grandfather showers her with respect and his love for her is openly shown. Although he is the Medicine Man of our people, to her he is also a loving and caring husband and family man.

We may stay in our village for many months at a time, but often we tend to wander across the vastness of the open land, which is our natural home. It is out there we find the true spark of adventure and freedom that runs through the blood of all our peoples, giving us our inner strength and resolve. Out in the wild we can let our soul mingle with the great forces of nature and in so doing, become more aware of our Mother the Earth and her unlimited power. It is after these long treks that we feel content to settle and rest for a while, back in this beautiful place in the bend of the river, known as Long Grass Creek.

It was here, my mother carried me inside her through the long dark winter months. She told me I helped to keep her warm during the intense cold of that particular winter, long ago. I had a twin ... but his journey into this world was difficult and he lived in his physical body for only a short while after his birth. I can still draw on that feeling of lying alongside him in the arms of our loving father. Neither of us was very strong and I think he decided to bequeath his strength to me, his elder brother, knowing on his return to Spirit we could still be close – even closer than if he had remained on the Earth. That close bond we have will never be broken, I am he ... and he lives in this world through me. We were of the same egg, shared the same space and even now, are of the same breath. Often I can sense his presence beside me. It reassures me when I am uncertain and comforts me whenever I am sad. He accompanies me when, to others, I appear to be on my own. His love lifts me up even higher than my friend the Hawk can fly. Sometimes I ponder on whether the Hawk and he ... are of the same.

My parents named me Two Wings and I am sure the love they continue to heap upon me is doubled by their knowledge of my brother's presence. They have told me I need never feel alone, for his spirit is strong and will always fly with mine. They say, when it is time for me to return to the Spirit Land, he will meet with me and guide me safely through. My mother has explained how, when I was being born, my father saw the wings of a great bird hovering above her and that later, as my twin brother ceased to be of this world, only the shadow of these wings flew away. My dear brother was gone, but not gone ... and so it is today. I bear my name with pride knowing I share part of it with him, for he was called Two Shadows. Sadly, my mother has never been able to carry another child, but one day I will present to her my future bride and she will then have the daughter she so desires.

I had an idyllic childhood for I loved the trees and woodlands and the forests beyond. My parents would smile at each other as they watched me running through the long grass with its beautiful fresh fragrance wafting all around. Often they would find me stretched out on my back, gazing up at the white clouds floating lazily across the sky. I enjoyed seeing their light wispy patterns change shape with the sudden movement of the wind over the prairie. I loved the earthy smell of the land upon which I lay and we laughed together when raindrops splashed down and fell onto my face. Whenever it was possible I would play in the trees at the edge of the forest. I could happily spend all day there, but my mother made me promise that every so often, I would return to let her know all was well. Even this was fun, for I imagined I was out on patrol and reporting in to a higher command. There were so many hidden trails I could follow, each one an adventure on its own. I knew where the deer rested and where young fox cubs could be found. I loved all the creatures, for they were my special friends with whom I shared this beautiful land and . . . like me, they were born free to roam therein.

I admired their ways and how swift they could move. How they would hide – and suddenly be gone. I watched them at play and envied their alertness and agility. I realized they were wise and so I learned from them. I learnt when to pause and stand very still or when to hide, or when to run. I learnt how to listen and breathe in each new smell. They taught me well. To look not just with my eyes but with my reasoning and thoughts. I would watch for many hours until I too could move as silently as they, for I discovered how to tread without leaving any mark or making a sound. I came to know where the different birds built their nests and what kind of cover they preferred and I also knew where their territories began and where they would end. I did my best to pass on this learning to my friends and we would play at stalking each other and anyone else who happened to wander by. We once saw a puma... but very quickly she was gone.

How much I enjoyed my childhood and the life we led and the precious memories of those days will always live in my heart. They remain forever bright and are there to sustain me when times appear harsh. They will never fade, for they are a gift to treasure and carry within. The riches of a man can indeed be counted by the recollections and thoughts which he holds deep inside him. One day, I know these memories will help me with the raising of my own family. I am so fortunate in that my loving parents are always there for me. My mother is tender and encouraging and my father is a kind and honest man. He and my uncles have taught me many things. My father himself, has spent much of his time and patience helping me to grow into the person I now am. His name is Grey Bear and he loves me as only a father can.   Maťhó Ȟóta

The Elders of our Tribe are wise and noble and speak words of great wisdom. They are respected by all and often converse with their fathers and grandfathers, even with the great-grandfathers. There is a wonderful calmness and serenity around them which brings about harmony and peace to our village. They instil a unity amongst us which, in turn, unites our families in a love and understanding of great magnitude and strength. We look to them for guidance and we savour their words. We try hard to follow their example of how to conduct ourselves in this world to which we now belong, knowing it is here we can discover the further lessons needed to advance our spirit within.

>>>> <<<<

"Just Something in the Air"

A wisp of smoke lies in the air
to linger for a moment there,
my senses rise . . . I stand and stare.

No cause it seems, no reason why
that soft-white haze should float on high,
I pause to think . . . at least, I try.

A fragrant perfume flows around
awakening memories profound,
my heart beats fast . . . I hear its sound.

There is no breeze - all is still
and yet this fragrance seems to fill
each part of me . . . I would it will.

For I can feel a tenderness
that brings to me such happiness,
as loving thoughts . . . my soul caress.

One day when this lies in the past
I'll hold the answers in my grasp,
for truly . . . I will seek and ask.

A gentle mist swirls in the air
and healing rays spread everywhere,
I share the peace . . . with those who care.

1.1.02

"Just the Legend of Tatanka – The Buffalo"

When I was a child, a long time ago,
I sat with my friends in the campfire's warm glow
and listened in awe to the words which poured from
the lips of an Elder . . . I never missed one,
for he was explaining how life had begun.

When our Ancestors came to this rugged land,
they found it so beautiful, spacious and grand,
from rolling prairies to wild mountains tall,
with woodlands and forests spread round like a shawl
'neath the sun's sparkling rays, giving energy to all.

Spring brought forth sweet blossoms, the summer bright flowers
and autumn showed colours that changed with the hours,
small streams ran through meadows while rivers so wide
roared through the canyons, touching each side
and waterfalls danced over rocks and hillside.

Our people were joyful, life was sublime
. . . but autumn was moving into winter time,
this world we had entered, though beautiful and bright,
was also quite savage within its own right –
the change of the seasons was causing such plight.

Although we admired all the beauty that flowed,
we'd taken for granted what Nature bestowed
'til the ground became hardened, then covered with snow
and lakes started freezing and blizzards would blow . . .
so the fruits and the berries no longer could grow.

The cold was intense, the days very short,
we felt that our life in a nightmare was caught,
most creatures perished or moved far away,
our Elders felt helpless, children cried in dismay . . .
and so to Wakan Tanka, we started to pray.

We asked to be saved from the misery around
- our bellies were empty, no food could be found,
but the Great Spirit listened as we called his name
and through his pure love . . . he banished our pain,
for from that moment onward, the buffalo came.

These mighty creatures we loved with our heart,
they fed us and clothed us and thus became part
of our culture and legends and the life that we knew.
Our tools and our weapons, our homes and toys too,
came from their huge bodies - our oneness just grew.

Yes, the buffalo came so that we may live,
offering the greatest gift they could give
and after each hunt our respect rang out clear
as we sent up our prayers for those lives gone from here
. . . wishing them a swift journey to the Spirit Sphere.

Tatanka is wise, powerful and strong,
he moves with the seasons - we follow along.
Out on the prairie we both like to roam
and because of his presence, our people have grown . . .
in this beautiful land, we are proud to call home.

13.09.10

CHAPTER THREE

Knowledge of the Whiteman

Like swarms of locust the Whiteman came, devouring the land without one kind thought. They wound their way over the open plains and through the canyons, across the grasslands and into the forests. They polluted the streams and rivers and invaded the sacred mountains. They did not seem to see the gentleness of Mother Earth and cared not about her carefully balanced ways, nor showed any concern for her beautiful features. They had even less respect for the many creatures who lived in this wilderness. The eyes of the Whiteman did not view the land as it was ... only how they wished it to be, for their ears never heard the cries of the wild and they did not listen to the words of its people. They sensed not the destruction in the changes they brought nor did they worry about the strange diseases they carried to another's body or mind. Their feelings never considered the true thoughts of those already here.

We of our kind, look upon this Earth as our mother and all the creatures who roam around and amongst us, are as brothers. We know that like man, they too are a part of the Great Spirit. To us, it is of no matter whether they are two-legged or four-legged, whether they crawl along the ground or fly upon the air. It makes no difference if they are of fur, skin, feather or scale. We love and admire them for they are indeed wise and unlike many men, they follow the Natural Laws of Nature. We try to copy their ways for we know they can teach us many things. Without the creatures, this world would be so empty. We would sorely miss their great beauty, their many different shapes, sizes and colours, their wild calls and uplifting songs . . . and that mystery and adventure which radiates from them. We, the Redman, cannot begin to understand how others do not appreciate these wonders of nature, for in doing so, they would surely recognise just how precious all God's creatures are. Without them, life would be doomed, for like our Elders teach us – we are all connected.

Sadly, the Whites simply rode in with their ambitions and greed. They wanted control of our people and when finally we were charged to reply, they sent the soldiers with their guns and weapons of huge force. They took our refusal to submit to their demands, to their ridicule of our ways and beliefs and their desecration of our Mother the land . . . as a proclamation of war. I feel they never really wanted to talk. They had decided in their far-off towns – that we were to go. They flattened our villages and murdered our kind and when we offered them peace, they returned our offer with lies. They hunted without reason, simply to kill . . . and of all the creatures to suffer the most, it was the noble buffalo whom they wantonly attacked. Their massive herds were mindlessly slaughtered, without even a second thought and with no pity shown to their young. Their blood stained the grasses and dust of the open plains and never again did the heavens echo to their thunderous roar, for the prairie was changed. The Whiteman laid monstrous tracks across the ground, which carried the Iron Horse from the east and from the west, until the Great Plains were cut into two. The home of our forefathers was ravaged by their stone-built towns and wooden shacks and the air was filled with 'strange wires of sound'. They blasted the rocks and felled thousands of trees until the land was scarred forever . . . the mighty beasts all gone.

Where was the reasoning, where was the cause? Oh yes, they found their answers in their blind quest for gold, but did they never consider the result of their actions? Why did they not understand the Natural Laws? How could they not know that what they did to others would one day be returned to them and that their spirit would suffer for the wrong they had done. They spoke of their God, but what kind of god encourages them to not only hurt another, but also to damage themselves? We know our spirit light is affected by the way we live here and that on returning to the Spirit Realms, we will see whether our soul shines any brighter or is dulled. We know we will be with like-minds and suffer the consequences of our worldly actions. If we have tried to be fair in our ways and respected the Earth and all therein, then when we move forth we will be with our Ancestors in those wild and wondrous places where our spirit can fly free. We will again walk with our loved ones who have travelled ahead and meet with those animal friends, whose companionship and loyalty we have continued to hold in our heart. Our spirit will be blessed with a beauty far beyond the beauty we have experienced and enjoyed in the forests, mountains and open grasslands of this our earthly home and we shall live forever in the memories of those whose love we share.

Yes, some of our Braves did take the hair of the Whiteman and yes, it was wrong – very wrong, but this was not before the Whiteman had taken to scalping those of our kind. To them it was a macabre game, often to see how many each could collect … and even to receive payment for their awful deeds, from their so-called 'betters'. Our people were not right to also do this dreadful thing, but these were young men who had seen their own wives, mothers and sisters, even their daughters brutally mutilated and abused. How would you, yourself, have reacted in such circumstances? When wrong is done to you it does not make things right by doing wrong to another, but grief and anger are both very powerful emotions and when put together, can be almost impossible to bear. Reason seems to be lost as clear thinking is diminished. Revenge then storms in and yet another destructive and powerful emotion is set free. My heart cries out for those of my people who fell to this depth. How deeply I mourned for them because of the darkness cast upon their spirit. What they had done they would have to account for, the hurt they gave out would be returned to them. There can be no excuses . . . to hurt another thing, be it man or creature or our Mother the Earth, is wrong. However, I do feel certain they will have since made amends for those things which should never have happened and that they are now free from their self-imposed suffering. I am sure their spirits will again be shining bright and that they are walking with our Ancestors, in those Realms of Light.

When we are gone from this earthly life the progression of our spirit continues. We are taken over that Great Divide by friends who have already journeyed forth. They reach out to guide us safely into the Spirit Lands. They help us to settle, as we re-adjust our vibrations to those higher and faster frequencies which our spirit works on, it having now been freed from the heaviness of the physical body which is left behind. Time is of no consequence and distance is no longer measured in miles, but with a quickness of thought. Depending on the way we pass from our life here, we will almost definitely need a time for healing . . . a healing of the mind. We will then spend time in our own spiritual homes, rejoicing in the company of those with whom we are reunited. We will enjoy the hopes we have carried with us, those innermost dreams which have stayed locked away for so long. Eventually we will be faced with the lives we have led and we will either benefit from the good we have shown, or we will feel the results of any suffering we have caused. No one escapes, for true justice is brought about through our own conscience being our judge. Our thoughts can no longer be hidden and our thinking is as the spoken word. If we did give out hurt, it is now returned to us and our pain is multiplied by how many it has touched. Likewise, if we were kind to others . . . then kindness is now known.

There also comes a time when we realise how we wish to put to use the experiences we have had in our material lives and share any knowledge gained. Many of my people have been allowed to 'return' and converse with the Earth-plane by learning how to control and lower their spirit vibrations and tune in to Earth's slower frequency. First we learn to communicate with those like ourselves . . . perhaps through the visions we send to the Medicine Man, or with the wisdom we impart in the minds of the Elders. We sit here, in our Circles of Light, so we may be able to talk with those of your world, even though many years have passed and our tribes are almost gone. We are both pleased and honoured to work with those who help us draw near, those people who are conscious of the spiritual gifts present in each one, those who understand how we are all Spirit, no matter who or what we are, or where we may abide. We try to bring forth more awareness of the peace and harmony found in the natural world and share our thoughts about the healing which is there for all, together with the cures found in the various potions and balms, used by our own Medicine Men.

We who have travelled on, still love Mother Earth and are drawn to those in whose memories we now live. We wish to help others to appreciate their lives and the beauty of *their* world. We know how, with loving thoughts, spirit can blend and so we say to those in your sphere . . . "Your spirit is there within your body while mine is alive and living here, but nought can stop both working together, if love and sincerity walk hand in hand with an awareness of mind." These are teachings from

Spirit – and thus it was taught in my village and to those of my kind.

I was ten years old when I had my first experience of losing someone through 'death'. It was the passing of a friend who was the same age as myself. I had always known how our body is but a shell, a covering which carries our spirit while it lives here on Earth. I also knew that our spirit is the 'real us' which continues to live on. As with other children before me, I was brought up with this understanding . . . an understanding of how we are all part of the Great Spirit and therefore a part of each other and indeed, of all living things. Death held no fear for me. Even at my tender age, I knew it could only happen to the physical part of a person and that our spirit itself, lives on for all time. However, it was not until I saw an 'empty' body devoid of life, its spirit flown, that I realised just how true this was, for on seeing his body – I knew it was no longer him.

My friends and I were playing quite happily by a bend in the river. We had been reminded many times to be careful of the fast-flowing currents found in the waters there and we were fully aware of what we could and could not do. We had even explained to the younger children how the water would be flowing very strongly beneath the surface, just out of view. We truly believed we were being so sensible on that fateful day. There had though, been a bad storm two nights before and the river was now swollen, the surrounding rocks lying quite low. We noticed the water was higher and therefore we moved further along the riverbank, to a place we thought we knew well. What we had not taken into account was how the swollen flood water could affect the normally slow current in this quieter part of the river.

I recall it was very hot that day and without exception, we all decided to cool ourselves by taking a swim, just as we had done for many summers past. We were splashing about in the water and generally enjoying ourselves lazing on the bank, when one of us happened to notice that White Star's dog was barking at the river's edge. He seemed to be very agitated, pawing at the water ... and then suddenly he sat down and started to howl. This caught the immediate attention of us all and to our horror, we realised White Star was no longer among our band. We called out to him, but in our hearts we already knew something was terribly wrong. One of us ran to fetch the men. Our first thought was to wade out into the river but our second thought made us hesitate, for we suddenly wondered why it was, that White Star's dog had stayed on the bank, instead of venturing in. Surely there must be a good reason. We pondered this for only a moment, for we knew his natural instincts were far better than ours and so we decided he must have sensed danger lying ahead. I also think he knew that if *he* had bounded into the fast-flowing water, *we* would almost certainly have followed. All these things were running through my mind as we looked helplessly at one another, each one feeling more and more desperate about what might have happened to White Star.

By now a number of our fathers had appeared and at that same moment, one of our group shouted out from further along the riverbank. We could see he was pointing to some large rocks near the water's edge and scrambling towards them, we found ourselves looking down on the crumpled body of our missing friend. It was as though a great silence enfolded us. Everyone, man and child alike, felt stunned. We stood there for quite a while, not moving at all, each person sending forth their own thoughts. Even the air itself seemed to stand still. It was at this time I clearly remember thinking how his body looked different, as if empty ... and I knew his spirit was no longer there. Closing my eyes and breathing in deeply, I sent him my love.

Evening was falling when our fathers gathered us together and spoke softly to us. They said there was no blame to be attached to anyone, for the swollen river had caused fast underwater currents to occur in places where usually, there were none. They explained how all would mourn for our departed friend. They gently told us that although everyone was extremely sad because his physical form had gone, we must remember how his spirit was now in a far better land. They did not want us to continually wrap sorrow and gloom around ourselves, for then we would dim the light of *our* spirit and in turn, this could prevent his spirit from joining with ours. He would feel our sadness and this would affect his peace of mind. We had to stay strong, not just for ourselves, but for the sake of our friend. We needed to grieve ... but then we must put his happiness before our grief, casting our own sadness aside. We should all be joyful his spirit was free.

His close family however, would grieve for twelve full moons and usually his sister would cut short her hair, but because of her young years, their father stepped in to take her place and instead would cut his. White Star had been a bright boy, wise beyond his years and always full of fun. He had enjoyed making others laugh and therefore, in order to remain true to his memory ... we vowed we should always smile when thinking of him. My father reminded me how the purpose of everyone's pathway is to progress their soul. To achieve physical awareness we must experience life in a physical world and for some people, their journey through this life may only need to be short, their worldly lessons few. Some are born on this Earth to help others to learn and maybe White Star's life was to provide lessons for those whom he knew. He had certainly made others happy in his short span of years and even his death could be a vital lesson, which we needed to go through.

I was comforted by my father's words, for although I felt extremely sad, I knew White Star would feel content to be back in his spirit home. I kept thinking about what he had told me only a few days before. He had confided how, on settling down to sleep one night, he suddenly awoke, for he sensed someone had entered his family's tipi. He could hear everyone else sleeping soundly and so he looked up and on doing this, he plainly saw the outline of an elderly woman standing nearby. He said that standing next to her...he could see me. He related how he felt quite at ease for the feelings he had were good, but while softly calling my name he blinked and both myself and the old woman were gone. Strangely, he did not ask for my opinion and so I said nought. However, I had no doubt at all that it was not myself, but the image of my twin brother, whom he had seen. The old woman, I felt sure, must have been one of his great grandmothers whom he had yet to meet. At the time I decided the reason for this happening was perhaps that he and I were to become even closer friends, but now there were other ideas which came into my mind. Now he was in Spirit, I knew we could be closer than we had ever been before...and if he was with my brother, it meant it would be easier for this to be so. I have continued to send him my love and I know he often draws near, especially when I need cheering up.

Love is to be found in many forms and in many ways – but the love of Spirit is the most powerful love of all. Although every person and each living thing is unique, a special oneness runs through everything...for all are a part of the Great Spirit, who moves within.

>>>> <<<<

"Just the Lament of the Redman"

Like a swarm of locust the Whiteman came
and brought with him nothing but sorrow and pain,
treating all those before him with utter contempt
as deeper and deeper his wagon trains went –
across the prairie, the land of our birth,
plundering the mountains, the valleys, the earth.
He uprooted the woodlands, he killed all he saw,
the beaver, the bear, the wild forest boar,
he massacred the buffalo, roaming so free,
their great mighty herds . . . we no longer see.
He took what he wanted, gave nought in return,
he lied to our people, our villages burned.

How can such destruction come forth from his Soul
did he never look further . . . see life as a whole,
could he not understand that all he gave out
would one day return, without any doubt
and how, when he passed over his spirit would show
the true light of his nature - these horrors to know,
for the hurt and the fear which he once spread around
would be there to torment him, his thoughts now impound.
Natural Law is unfaltering, totally fair,
the terror he caused . . . he would thus have to bear,
no-one can escape for the truth is made clear
when the deeds which they did - before them appear.

His actions were brutal, his word quite untrue,
ambition and greed was all that he knew,
for our Mother the Earth he held no respect . . .
he seemed to be blind to 'cause and effect'.
The streams were polluted, the hillsides were scarred,
most creatures he slaughtered, each horse he rode hard.
His living was centred on only himself,
he cared not for others, his only thought - wealth,
but how could he not know that ill-gotten gain
would crush his own spirit, bring nothing but pain.
Yes, the damage he caused left such sorrow behind
for the hundreds of Tribes that were once of my kind.

30.5.02

"Just Suitably Dressed for the Journey"

Look upon life as a journey
with lessons that need to be known
and know when this journey is ended -
only then will you reach your true home,
know that your body is simply
a garment to wear on your way
and when it is no longer needed . . .
like a coat you can cast it away.

This journey through life is for knowledge,
different lessons are shown at each stage,
from when we are tiny as children
until we have entered old age,
yet some shed their coat fairly early
because they have worn it before
but still had some room in their pockets . . .
for what they had not learnt for sure.

Others whose coats weigh so heavy
- full of the knowledge therein,
are often allowed to discard them
not long after lessons begin,
but know that whatever its colour,
the size, or the shape, or the make,
the coat that is given unto us . . .
is right for the journey we take.

6.6.95

CHAPTER FOUR

Two Memorable Events

I met my soul mate one beautiful sunlit evening down by the river. She was sitting on a grassy mound near to a waterfall. She saw me instantly and I could tell from her expression that we were 'of the same'. Her eyes were bright and sparkled with fun and sincerity. She had long black hair which was thick and shiny and I knew it would smell as sweet as the scented pine. It was parted in the middle and hung down in two loose plaits, one each side of her face. Her skin was smooth and looked so soft – and I also knew it too, would smell divine. She sat quite still for awhile, I think secretly pondering on what to do next. Eventually, she arose and stood shyly before me, looking quite delightful in her white deer-skin dress, fringed at the hem and around the short sleeves. Her body was slim and she wore a thin belt, interwoven with tiny coloured beads, which showed off her small waist. The braids from her moccasins were criss-crossed up and around her legs and I can clearly remember thinking – how small were her feet. Her mouth was slightly turned up at each corner and as she looked innocently at me, her smile turned into a cheeky grin. I loved her then . . . and I have continued to love her ever since. Her name was 'Running Water'.

She too had been born in Long Grass Creek and was just a year younger than myself. Her family were friendly and well liked by all. They lived at the far end of our village, where their tipi was just out of sight from that of my own family. I had never really taken notice of her before . . . although as young children we had probably shared in the same games and been taught by the same teachers. While she quietly stood there beneath the trees, I slowly moved a little further along the pathway, from around the boulders where I had first appeared into view. Walking slowly towards her, I found this time . . . it was *I* who was wondering what to do or say. I muttered 'hello' and asked if I could sit on the mound, where she herself had been resting. To my great delight, she sat back down too. My heart started beating so fast and so loud, that I thought she would surely notice, as women do, but to my great relief – if she had, she said nothing. She seemed to be quite relaxed and gradually I felt more at ease myself, as we now laughed at the fish jumping in the stream and at the breeze blowing my long hair across my chin. It was a blending of spirits, or perhaps I should say . . . a re-union of Souls.

From that moment onward, we were hardly ever apart. When her daily chores were finished she would meet me by the same falls – it had become our special place. During the times I was away from her, I would always hold the image of our meeting there, in my mind. We spent the rest of the summer in perfect bliss and harmony, enjoying each other's company and getting to know better each other's ways. Our parents were as happy for us as we could have wished and we spent time in each family's tipi. She had a younger sister named 'Morning Mist' who used to tease me and in return, I would chase her around the trees and across the small streams. She would shriek loudly and all three of us would finish in a heap on the ground, the two girls giggling and hugging one another in their own girlish way. We were truly happy and it felt so good to be alive.

Our love blossomed and by the time the first snows came, we were quite inseparable. She was fascinated by my friend the

Hawk and I was so proud and pleased when he allowed her to stroke his feathers and touch the top of his head. Perhaps I was even jealous of the attention she paid him, or maybe of the friendship he formed with her – but these words I only say in jest. It was a relief to see them bond so well, but then ... how could they fail to do so? Knowing and believing what I did, I should have known for certain that they would accept each other. My mother and father both came to adore her – and she them. She was indeed, the daughter my mother had always yearned for. They would chatter together and deliberately share secrets in front of me, which at times made me blush. Then they would gently taunt me with their whisperings, but all this was done in good fun. Each really enjoyed the other's company and they often took long walks together, through the woodland. On returning home, their hand-woven baskets were full of various flowers, herbs and berries, which they divided between our families.

From the age of thirteen, Running Water had been brought up by her father, with the help of her paternal grandmother. This came about because, in the late summer of her twelfth year, her mother had quite suddenly fallen ill. My grandfather, being the Medicine Man, did what he could to help both her mother and her family. However, in the following Spring her mother's spirit slipped quietly away, to resume its life in the next world. Although the prayers and healing balms did not mend her body, they had certainly helped her spirit to travel peacefully over, for in those last months prior to her passing, her mother's pains had gradually ceased and even though she remained weak, her mind was at ease. This was a difficult time for Running Water but like myself, she was very aware of the reality of spirit. She knew how her beloved mother would always be there if she needed her and that she could and would, draw close with a gentle touch or reassuring word. Her father had never taken another wife, so her widowed grandmother lovingly stepped in to fill the gap left in their family life. I was already thinking that now . . . Running Water would also have me to love and care for her.

The time was approaching when the Elders of our people were preparing to visit the sacred place of our Ancestors, high up in the Black Hills. There was a tangible air of anticipation flowing through the village, for my friends and I, along with others, were eagerly hoping we would be invited to accompany our fathers on this most important quest. It would certainly be a great honour to take part – but it was obvious that some would need to stay behind, to take care of the women and children. Of course, I could not help wanting to be one of those who would go. For the next few weeks the main topic of conversation was to do with the journey which lay ahead. Everybody in the village became involved. Even the young children were instructed as to what was about to take place. It was important they understood such things, for it helped them to know more about their Ancestors from long ago. They sent out prayers to the Great Spirit, asking that their love be safely carried on the wind, at the same time as the Elders journeyed forth over the open plains, to the foothills beyond. They knew all thoughts were a living energy and could travel freely between this sphere and those other spheres hidden just out of view of the physical eye. They already knew some of the ways of spirit and now they needed to learn more about the ways of our people.

The women were busy making certain items of clothing which would be worn for such a special occasion. They also supervised the young girls on the baking of small cakes of bread. These were to be taken along with meat, which first had to be dried. This food would only be used when the men were high up in the mountains, for we never hunted in the Black Hills . . . in this sacred place, all were free. The young men were given the important task of preparing the horses, again under the close supervision of their fathers. Our ponies needed to be exercised more than usual and given extra food to strengthen them for the journey. Their coats were carefully groomed and then painted with various colours and designs. They were all thoroughly examined and we made sure their hooves were in fine shape. Their beautiful thick manes were plaited with beads and coloured braid and we also attended to their tails, although these were always left flying free.

All this activity drew to a climax two days before the event was due to take place. A special meeting around the campfire was set up and everyone was invited to attend. It was held on a new moon, when the sky was so clear that every star in the heavens seemed to be looking down. The air was quite still and even the wolves stayed silent. Our Medicine Man looked very impressive in his full tribal dress and I felt proud to be one of his grandsons. He seemed to dance even more in tune with the sacred drum and the flames of the fire, for tonight he was accompanied by our noble Braves. They too were decorated in arm and anklet bands and colourful braid. Our Elders wore their tribal bonnets and these magnificent head-dresses stood out in the soft moonlight. What a grand night it was, as the lingering smell of the lit sage floated all around on the evening air.

At the height of the ceremony the names of those who had been chosen to go, were called out. Every person was listening intently, including myself. Following each single drum beat a name was announced: Blazing Bow ... Red Flame ... Running Dog ... Speaks with Ravens ... Green Shoots and so forth until at last, with sheer joy I heard my own name called ... Two Wings. After that, everything seemed to become a blur. I did try to keep my concentration, so as to be aware of who else was being summoned. I turned to look at Running Water, whom I could see was feeling so pleased for me. I was determined to do well on this journey and in so doing, gain even more of her love and respect. I could see my dear mother wiping a tear from her eye and I sensed her reaching out to me. I spoke subconsciously to my twin brother... "I have made it. I am going on this long trek to be that little closer to our past. Travel with me, even though you are already there." This, together with my meeting and falling in love with Running Water, were two of my first most memorable occasions, for as I have already said... I was only just starting out on my pathway to becoming a man.

I thought I would never sleep that night for there were so many things swimming in my head and yet, as soon as I closed my eyes, I was no longer in our tipi, but drifting far away. We all travel in our sleep state, back into the land of Spirit. More often than not, we cannot recall these astral journeys and on our awakening again in this world, we then struggle to make sense of those vague thoughts left lingering in our mind. Sometimes I think how sad this is... for I would dearly love to return with the memories and learning we receive from there. I know our body needs to sleep, but I truly believe there is yet another reason why we slumber. I believe sleep helps our spirit within to be refreshed, by keeping it in touch with its previous surroundings and allowing it to meet up again with spirit guides and helpers. I am convinced we travel over there to enable our loved ones to be close to us on their side of life, for they miss our presence too. The Spirit World is just as real and as solid to them as our World is to us, for their vibrations match those in which they now live.

When someone leaves their earthly existence, their spirit gradually adjusts to the quicker frequencies which are over there. I sincerely wish all people could be aware of how natural the passing from this world to the next world, really is. It is sad to lose the physical part of a person whom you have known and loved, but the body is nothing without the spirit which moved therein, for that spirit is the true person who spent time with you in the physical sphere. When it is time for the spirit to move back into its original abode, then we should feel happy – for it has only returned home. It no longer required the lessons which are to be found in this world and so it needed to be freed from its earthly shackles, in order to forward its learning and keep its spark bright.

The Great Spirit is a part of all and we should continually strive to progress in the right way, so that one day we will be ever nearer to his all-loving light. With our Mother the Earth we need to blend in a positive way and then rejoice in the knowledge we have gained. We should be prepared to listen with open minds to the wisdom received from those who speak forth to our spirit within, so that we in turn can help others along their pathway of life. As lives come and go, so the great wheel of life rolls forever onward, moving over the rough and the smooth, into experiences good and bad, through the light and the dark, collecting on its way both wisdom and foolishness, harmony and chaos. It will never stop, for like all things circular, it has no beginning and no end. Life, as we see it . . . 'just is'.

"Just Special Memories"

As the stars shine bright in the fragrant night
and the moon above speaks of young love . . .

I can recall, just for a while,
the moment I first saw your smile,
it warmed my heart, my senses stole,
it changed my life . . . it touched my soul
for in that instant when we met
it was like time had been re-set,
our thoughts enclosed within a haze
- we softly held each other's gaze.
It seemed with ease we could both trace
the outline of the other's face,
from memories locked inside our heart
. . . special memories, that impart
awareness of a different kind,
lingering there, deep in our mind.
Somehow, it clearly seemed to me
I knew you well - yet could this be!
Unless it had been in a dream
or from a far off distant scene,
another time, an unknown place . . .
my reasoning would not keep pace.
Though I could not remember more
I knew we had unlocked a door
which opened up a stream of love,
flowing from the heavens above.

This power of love just grew and grew
as we stood in each other's view,
I sensed I'd never be the same
- your tender look had lit a flame
that would forever gently burn
within my inner-most concern.
Never again could I just be
a single being . . . only me,
for while I watched you standing there
I knew my life with you I'd share.
There was a bond wrapped round us two
that no-one ever could undo,
it came from very far away
and drew us closer day by day
unleashed from oh, so long ago,
a time we did no longer know,
but now that time was here again
renewed within love's constant flame.

The moon and stars sparkle anew, whene'er I pause
. . . and think of you.

25.7.97

"Just Learning to Be"

Show me a child who's surrounded in love
and I'll give you the adult whose outlook is good.

Show me a child who learns to be fair
and I'll give you the adult who's willing to share.

Show me a child whose mind is kept free
and I'll give you the adult who's good company.

Show me a child who enjoys simple things
and I'll give you the adult whose soul often sings.

Show me a child whose smiles rarely cease
and I'll give you the adult whose thoughts are of peace.

Show me a child who is offered his say
and I'll give you the adult who speaks of fair play.

Show me a child who knows of respect
and I'll give you the adult who gives of his best.

Show me a child who is taught to be kind
and I'll give you the adult who's honest of mind.

Show me a child whose efforts gain praise
and I'll give you the adult who'll try in all ways.

Show me a child who is happy to be
and I'll give you the adult who brings harmony.

Show me a child who knows of himself
and I'll give you the adult who has inner wealth.

30.11.01

CHAPTER FIVE

The Black Hills . . . He Sapa

Eventually the day of our departure arrives and as the dawn starts to break and the sun rises majestically above the far horizon, we slowly ride out from our village. Our ponies look sleek, with their coats clean and shining and the heat from their bodies is visible in the crisp, light air. They are eager to move. We pat their strong necks as they tread gracefully over the firm ground, their heads held proud and high. The morning dew is fresh and their hooves leave glistening imprints on the grass, which then slowly fade and disappear. Rays of sunshine spread out across the prairie, as if they are lighting up a pathway for our horses to follow. Our womenfolk stand in little clusters, having bade us farewell and our view of them grows ever smaller as we move further away. We are riding through the tall grasslands towards the Great Plains. The grass sways very gently in the soft breeze. The smell of the earth beneath us is good and the warm sunlight upon our backs is quite invigorating.

As we reach the bend in the river, we know we are moving out of sight of our village. We think about our families, who will now return to their tipis and sleep for a little longer. When they re-awaken the whole village will once again be alive with activity. While the women cook and our children play, the men left behind will welcome the new day. We will stop to respectfully acknowledge the Sun when we are out on the plains. The world feels right as we move with joy through the grandeur of our homeland, this land which is so much a part of us. Far in the distance we can see the rugged outline of the mountains, to which we ride. The splendid high tops of the Black Hills are just visible and we think about our forefathers, whose sacred place this is. We reflect on how they would have ridden, just like we are doing on this bright summer morning, to pay respect to their fathers before them – and we know they ride with us now. We feel comfortable in the knowledge that one day, our own bones will be placed in the lofty peaks of these beautiful tree-covered mountains we love. When we are freed from this earthly body, what better place to return to ... than He Sapa. Death is only a step across that great divide between here and the Spirit Sphere.

My Hawk sits contentedly on the mane of my pony and I note in my mind how ordered his feathers lie. He is a handsome bird and I respect and love him dearly. How old is he now? Can it be only two years since I first found him? What a great friendship we share. I sincerely hope he is as happy as I am. Suddenly, he shuffles his feet and ruffles his feathers, as if he is aware of what I am thinking and then quite effortlessly, he flies up into the blue sky. I watch him as he skims over my pony's head, barely missing his ears, but my horse knows this unusual friend of mine has never yet hurt him with his sharp talons. This powerful bird circles round, gliding over the top of the long grass, his wings fully spread, skilfully playing on the warm pockets of air rising from the ground. He is extremely agile and it is a pleasure to watch as he now soars upwards. He too is enjoying the total freedom which lies before and around us, he too, feels good with the sun on his back and the land spread out beneath him. He circles our ponies again and again, before swooping up even higher ... and for a little while, I lose sight of him as he continues to soar into the heavens above. Without any warning and with hardly any noise, he returns to settle once more upon the thick braided hair of my trusty steed.

We continue quietly onwards, each man carrying his own thoughts within his mind. Thoughts of this journey which lies before him, thoughts of the life flowing on in the village we are leaving behind. Thoughts of his children and the woman he loves. We are slowly moving out onto the Great Plains which now stretch far ahead, until one of our Chiefs raises his hand and we slow to a stop. It is time to dismount and pay homage to the sun and give thanks in appreciation of the light and energy it sends, warming our hearts as well as our bodies. Kneeling upon the soft earth with our backs straight, we look into the vastness of the sky above, stretching out our arms to embrace its beauty, before lifting them up high. It is here we wish to talk with the Great Spirit who gives life to all things. We see white clouds drifting peacefully by, as we send forth our love. Thus we greet the sun who has awakened the day and welcome the soft cool breeze and sweet-smelling air. Each one of us feels privileged to share in the goodness that is swirling around.

We honour the land and the Great Spirit therein, together with our Mother the Earth. We send out grateful thoughts for all the gifts given to us — each breath that we take and the natural healing received from the trees, flowers and herbs. We are truly thankful for the refreshing rain and for the peaceful harmony we feel when viewing the high mountains and green prairie. We ask that we stay faithful and true, so the flame of our spirit is rekindled anew. We know by nourishing its light within us, we gain the strength of our forefathers, who reach out to us in love. We ask for our own love to be used as a healing balm, for all those who may need its upliftment and calm.

>> <<

Back in the village, Running Water cannot help feeling sad, now that Two Wings is away. She is missing him far more than she anticipated, yet although her heart is heavy, she feels happy for him. She knows how much joy it brought to him when he was chosen to ride on this journey to the Black Hills. She tries to make time pass more quickly by finding extra work to do, but it is to no avail – each hour seems to go so slowly. Both her days and nights are spent dreaming of the love they share, trying to imagine what he is doing at any given moment, for this helps her to feel that little bit closer to him. His absence has certainly made her realise just how much they have become a part of each other, for it is as though a piece of her is now missing. She eagerly sends out more thoughts to him, knowing that he in turn, will be thinking of her.

Whenever possible, she takes time to walk into the group of tall trees behind the waterfall where they first met. Ever since she was a young child, she has always found a great comfort in being amongst the foliage there. She now slowly breathes in the freshness of the woodland air and is aware of the scented pine needles blending in with the aroma of the ferns and flowers, which are growing densely all around. The early morning mist drifts silently between the trees, as the sun's warming rays start to gradually filter down through the higher branches, reaching out overhead. Drops of dew sparkle on the many different shaped leaves, while spiders' webs shimmer softly in the haze. The air here is so fragrant and birdsong echoes through the thicket and across the many glades.

Running Water quietly sits down upon a large bough that has fallen to the ground. As her fingers tenderly caress the blades of grass growing beside her, she is fully conscious of the natural vibrations around. Leaning against the tree's broad trunk and tilting her head gently backwards until it rests on the bark, she immediately feels an energy which is quite profound. Silently she sends out her thanks for the healing being given and asks that the tree retains its own strength. Her body is totally relaxed and her mind at ease. In this peaceful state she senses her passed loved ones are drawing near and welcomes the chance to be closer to them. Blending into their love, all sadness is soon forgotten. Her awareness deepens as she shares precious memories with them, until the joyous sounds of the children playing in the village eventually bring her back into this world. Standing up and stretching slowly in the warmth of the sunshine, her heart is refilled with happiness. She breathes in the healing radiating from this part of the woodland which means so much to her – and to Two Wings. Feeling refreshed and much more contented, she carefully picks her way through the undergrowth and steps out of the leafy thicket and across the small stream. Inside her, she carries the love and calmness she has again been fortunate to receive. Running Water quietly returns to her family's tipi, now quite eager to face the new day.

>> <<

I am also happy, for after travelling for two days and resting through each night, we reach the foothills of the sacred mountains and make camp at sunset on the third day. We settle ourselves next to a stream and sit quietly to watch as the last rays of the sun move quickly up and over the hilltops. Our horses graze in the coolness of the evening and my Hawk is busily preening his feathers, having eaten his fill. The unmistakable sound of trickling water nearby immediately reminds me of the waterfall where I love to sit with Running Water . . . and I send out special thoughts for her. The moon looks bold and clear, while each star dances so brightly. The conversation between my friends gradually becomes less and less, as tiredness sets in and sleep overcomes us all. Tomorrow will be good.

Next morning, as we are moving further into the Black Hills, it becomes a truly amazing experience, for the higher we climb, the more at one we feel with our surroundings. We can see the jagged peaks above and the vibrant green of the trees around and below us. It is as though our body, as well as our spirit, is now a part of all this beauty. We breathe in the fresh mountain air, allowing it to course through us and awaken those Spiritual Centres hidden deep within each one. These seven main energy points, which swirl unseen inside every living thing, are the link between the Earth body and our spirit form. They are finely balanced and just like our physical organs, need to be nourished and kept 'in tune'. When the senses of the spirit are roused, they heighten spiritual awareness and help us to blend mind and body alike. It serves us well to know that the power of the mind determines the strength of the body and how it functions ... but we must also remember how the condition of the body can affect our thinking. We need to stay alert and positive at all times, looking after our spiritual-self as well as our physical one.

Our senses are now fully motivated as we encounter the strong presence of our Ancestors who have drawn so close. What love enfolds us as we slowly press on and how great our own sensitivity has become. Relating to the thoughts being sent from those left behind in our village and at the same time blending with the energies that flow, we offer prayers and respect while scattering our love upon the air. We lose ourselves in the quiet and in the harmony, each man with his own thinking, yet each of a similar mind. Everyone starts to feel a great surge of well-being as we recognise how it is our oneness of thought which is helping our spirits to bond. The decision is made to dismount and rest. How long we stop and stay is of no importance, for time ceases to be ... it no longer exists. Immersed in the peace, we sit with our eyes closed, our inner-selves fully entwined with the rhythm of our spirit, completely lost in the pure love we feel. Now we are truly amongst those of our people who have moved on.

I could happily remain like this for several hours, but then suddenly, yet quite gently, we are made aware of a cold wind. It moves over our faces, encouraging us to breathe in deeply and hold our breath, until slowly exhaling. This we repeat once more, before attempting to open our eyes. No matter how slowly this is done, we still react to the brightness of the colours spread around us. We look at each other and smile, as if meeting for the first time after a long absence. For a moment or two, nothing is said. All remain silent. Then we embrace ... and grasping each other by the forearm and patting one another's shoulders, we share in the spiritual joy we have known. Eventually, everybody settles down again for the final meal of the day.

After meditating I have always felt ready to eat, but now it comes into my mind that the sensation I have in my 'gut' is not one of hunger, but probably something quite different. I begin to realise this 'feeling' is coming from my solar plexus, the area just below my ribs – and of the seven main energy points, it is the one at the solar plexus we are most likely to feel. When opening up in meditation, this feeling is more acute. It surprises me I have never thought about this before, because it helps me to appreciate how there is more to my 'hunger' than I first understood. I smile again, this time to myself, for it certainly sheds new light on the expression – 'having a gut feeling'.

Knowing how my spirit and body interconnect, I spend some time thinking about these spiritual centres deep inside my earthly shell. I reason how the brow centre, or third eye, must be the next most defined one. I've been taught to use these seven centres to reach out to the faster vibrations of spirit, concentrating first on the red colour at the base of my spine before moving up to the orange of the lower body. From there I move to the yellow of the solar plexus and then to the green of the heart. Next comes the blue of the throat and the purple of the brow. Finally, I reach the lilac or white of the higher self, just above the top of my head. These rainbow colours glow inside each and everyone, yet because they are of our spirit, many will never see them – but all should know they are there.

My thoughts are suddenly interrupted by the touches I feel on my elbow. It is my friend, Green Shoots. He is offering me some of the small cakes of bread and other food that is being passed around. I think again of Running Water and the others back home in our village ... and hope all is well. We are enjoying this journey into these sacred mountains, but we miss being with those left behind. Quietly I ask the Great Spirit for added protection to be placed around them while we are here, so far away. After another day spent in such lovely surroundings, the Elders announce it is time to return. Slowly we move down through the dark green forest to spend the night back in the foothills, before making the long trek home. All carry with them a mixture of feelings. Although obviously happy at the thought of seeing our families again, we are also sorry to be leaving this special place. We send more loving thoughts to our Ancestors and sincere thanks to the Great Spirit, for the beauty and inspiration found in these peaceful hills.

As we gradually leave behind the high peaks, the terrain opens up into wooded valleys and sweet-smelling meadows and we soon notice the presence of Tatanka, the Buffalo. The last time we met with our noble friend was many months ago, when we pursued him out on the Great Plains. Tatanka is a true friend, for without him those of our kind could not survive. We are forever grateful ... and being here with him now, allows us to sit and enjoy his greatness. He is indeed a mighty creature with his rugged coat draped over huge, powerful shoulders. His massive head is strong enough to clear away the deepest snow in the winter-time and his sure-footed thin legs keep his huge body perfectly balanced. Although he is of a great weight, he can still run far faster than any man – and indeed faster than many beasts, including the wolf. In the 1800s there were millions of buffalo and we could ride, hunt and live freely . . . for there were sixty million acres of land. Our people numbered hundreds of thousands and we were divided into around fifty different Tribes – all united by our respect for the land, our respect for Mother Earth.

In those now fast fading days, there were less than 20,000 whitemen living west of the Mississippi River. Perhaps it is best that at this moment in time I have no real understanding of what is to come . . . the horror and the tragedy that faces our Race, brought about by the greed and self-importance of others whose sole objective is to dominate and destroy. How wise is Spirit Law, the law which means our memory of what we are to learn and experience in this world, is wiped away while we live our lives here. How could we possibly bear the 'knowing' of future events when they encompass such suffering.

On returning to our village we are met first with greetings and then with questions. How was our journey? Did all go well? Were the spirits strong and our forefathers pleased? How did it feel and were we well fed? Our joy is shared over and over again, but this time with those whom we love here in this world. We are pleased they too feel uplifted. Yes, it has been a great experience . . . but it is good to return home! We have missed the company of our women and children and it is a pleasure to behold our tipis again. This has been a good year with almost constant sunshine – though still enough rain. The air is warm and yet fresh while the land is enriched and carrying a great abundance of natural wealth.

"Just an Early Morning Walk"

In a forest glade just out of view,
carpeted in morning dew,
she steps so easily o'er the ground . . .
her moccasins, making no sound
as through the thicket, lush and green,
where can be heard a gushing stream
- she moves along, quite serene.

With early sunbeams filtering through
from a sky so clear and blue,
she sits upon a grassy mound –
her mind at peace, her thoughts profound,
for safe within this restful scene
she opens up and in a dream . . .
shares words of truth with friends unseen.

These are those Spirits good and true
whom long ago she met and knew,
deep in the forest they abound
for here their healing powers are found.
She blends within their loving beam
- ever ready, ever keen
to learn more of life's natural theme.

From a forest glade, sparkling with dew,
she walks so quietly into view,
towards the tipis scattered round
where children play and run and bound.
Leaving the falls and small ravine
she crosses the meadow and the stream
- bringing back the love of those Supreme.

20.5.02

"Just the Prayer of a North American Indian"

I am part of all nature and
share as my home
the open prairie where buffalo roam,
I travel the Great Plains that
stretch ever far
and ride with my brothers 'neath
sun, moon and star.

'Tis dawn when our leader
raises one hand and
we slow to a stop without any command,
it is time to dismount and reach
out with our mind
and send loving greetings to
those of our kind.

We kneel on the earth, our
backs straight and high
and spread out our arms, raising them to the sky,
we look to the heavens with
white clouds above,
as we send forth our thoughts filled
with homage and love.

We acknowledge the sun as
he wakens the day
and welcome the wind and the breezes that play
on the sweet-smelling air rising
up from the ground,
sharing its goodness with
all those around.

We honour the land and our
Mother the Earth
and cherish the gifts we received at our birth,
each breath that we take, Nature's
great healing powers,
found high in the mountains, in trees,
herbs and flowers.

We ask that our thinking stay
faithful and true
to kindle the flame of our spirit anew,
nourishing its light with the
strength that we bear
. . . knowing our forefathers'
love is still there.

31.5.02

"Just an Indian's Journey Home"

Great Spirit guide me safe to Thee
as from my body I'm set free.
From Mother Earth I now depart
towards that land within my heart,
where buffalo roam constantly
on open plains and one can see
the buzzard flying in the sky,
o'er mountain ranges rising high,
the prairies and the tall green grass,
the pinewoods where the deer run fast
and flowing streams meandering through
the rocky canyons that I knew.
I hear the chanting once again
around the campfires friendly flame,
I see shapes dancing through the smoke
which swirls around them like a cloak . . .
Singing Bird and Silver Bow,
ancestors from long ago.

What rejoicing there will be
as I greet each family,
what excitement in my heart
now I can become a part
of all that's deep within my soul,
as distant memories unroll
and take me back to what I've known –
would once more be my spirit home.
Mighty Spirit, by thy hand,
I am at peace within this land.
I am the mountains which I see,
I am the river running free.
I'm in the rain, I'm in the breeze,
I can relate with simple ease
to all that is around me here –
we are as one within this Sphere.
Oh Great Spirit, let me be,
all which is a part of Thee
as now I cross that Great Divide . . .
to walk forever by Thy side.

1.7.95

CHAPTER SIX

Conflict with the Whiteman

As the village suddenly awakens to the shouts of its young men, Running Water immediately opens her eyes and jumps to her feet. However, before opening the flaps of her family's tipi, she stops and hesitates. Her father too has risen and he quietly cautions his daughter to stay still. Grandmother starts to stir and looks inquisitively up at them, concern showing on her normally placid face. Running Water is told to take care of her and of Morning Mist, her younger sister. Their father then moves swiftly but silently across to kiss each of them on the forehead. At the tipi doorway he reaches for his knife and lifting the flap, disappears outside into the early morning light. Running Water is troubled and unsure. She walks over to the frail form of her grandmother who is gently beckoning to her. The old lady is now propped up on one elbow, but still covered by the brightly patterned blanket wrapped around her beneath the warm buffalo robe. "We must be quiet..." she whispers to her grand-daughter, "very quiet and very still."

Running Water knows her instinctive curiosity is urging her to step out of their tipi to see what is happening, but a greater instinct takes over, one that warns her to remain hidden. She turns to Morning Mist who is only half awake and signals to her – she mustn't move, for she dare not chance her younger sister making any noise. Outside it has become extremely quiet. Not one dog is barking. Running Water knows they will have been taken to one side and ordered to lie down and stay silent. She kneels by the side of their grandmother and in the soft dim light surrounding them, reaches out for her hand...in a bid to soothe her. However, it is she who finds comfort in the warmth shining from her grandmother's eyes. Both are wondering what could be the cause of all this excitement. Has the Great Bear wandered into their village – but if this was so, they would hear his deep growls, while the dogs would be loudly barking and the men shouting. Morning Mist is clearly frightened, yet Grandmother has regained her composure and turning to her younger grand-daughter smiles...and nods her head reassuringly. This kindly old woman has a way of calming people by simply looking at them, for her expression is so full of love, it melts away any fears. The thin wrinkled lines on her forehead and around her face, speak not just of age, but of a deep wisdom lying within – a wisdom gained over many, many years.

Suddenly a shadow appears at the side of their tipi and the voice of Two Wings floats upon the air. Grandmother bids him enter and Running Water feels such relief in seeing him standing there. He asks them to dress quickly. Their Scouts have noticed others moving towards the village, completely unannounced. Two Wings then turns and goes out. Running Water is indeed quick to dress and as she steps into the cool morning air, she cannot know that it is the beginning of a great change for her people and those of her kind. Some of the younger Braves have been carefully positioned between the tipis, while others have spread out around their camp. The older men have gathered together and are talking in low voices with the Elders, who are sitting outside their lodges on the stony riverbank. The children have been kept inside. Two Wings and some of the other young men are told to take the ponies into the forest, where they will be safely hidden from sight.

>> <<

Those who are approaching are Cheyenne. Although they are friends of the Lakota, it is the custom for them to send two of their people ahead. When this is not done, we know something must be wrong and *they* will know we have understood . . . and therefore be on our guard. This happens without any words being said. As they ride into our village we can see the troubled looks upon their faces and sense the tension they carry with them. They quietly dismount and while their ponies are led away to be refreshed, they walk over to the Elders who are waiting to welcome them. The women of our Tribe have gathered together and have started preparing extra food for our visiting friends. For once, there is hardly any talk exchanged between them. This morning, all have their own thoughts, which they keep in their head. The feeling of anxiety is intense.

These Cheyenne have come from the lands stretching out to the east and they now tell of soldiers whom they have seen riding along the great river there, the river which is fed by many streams. The soldiers are camped in large numbers and next to their tents can be seen cannons on wheels. The atmosphere surrounding these military men is not good and an air of uncertainty flows through their camp. There are also reports of long columns of whitemen slowly moving into the foothills of the sacred mountains. They are digging up the ground and ravaging the streams, thus polluting the waters which flow from there. Many trees are being felled and many birds and creatures disturbed. There is talk they have found great wealth hidden in the Black Hills and we begin to realise the enormity of what is being said.

We know the Whites do not view wealth as seen through the eyes of the Redman. We have been told that when the Whiteman speaks of wealth, he does not refer to the beauty of

63

what lies around him, but only to what he can take for himself. We have heard about his greed for belongings and his desire to control those whom he sees. We already know how others are facing real hardship in the lands to the west ... those around the Powder River Basin and in the mountains of the Big Horn, as well as in areas to the north. There is mention of the soldiers being led by a man known as Yellow Hair, a powerful man who seems to enjoy war. We fear there are going to be terrible battles fought and the blood of both the Whiteman and Redman shed. The Chiefs and Warriors of many Tribes are uniting to face up to this threat. Red Cloud, *Mahpiya Luta*, who is one of the most trusted and respected Chiefs of the Lakota, is attempting to negotiate with the leaders of the Whites. He is a spokesman for us all and his wish and ours, is to try and secure peace. However, we do appreciate there are those amongst us who are not prepared to try, for times are extremely difficult and tempers are running high.

We are not afraid of the Whiteman – we are only afraid of the trouble he brings. We know that to the east great towns have risen up and that land has been taken from those of our kind. We have heard of villages being burned and their people cruelly slain. One day perhaps, the soldiers will come into our village, but if so, we hope it will be as a friend. We hope the great leaders of our Tribes will be able to help them understand how our people have roamed these open spaces for a long, long time, but have never tried to own the land. How can we? The land is our Mother and she is there for each and everyone ... and indeed for everything. We hope this thought will enter into the minds of the white people and that in their wisdom, they too will wish to find peace, for surely – there is room for all. We have been told there are some whitemen who respect the ways of nature and are true to the creatures and to the land, but we have also been told that their numbers are few. How unfortunate this is, for we could have walked as brothers through the vast wilderness which lies all around. Sadly it was not to be. The ones who were tolerant of our different ways were often rebuked by others of their kind. They were even punished and sometimes killed.

I fear for the Whiteman and the thoughts he has – and I fear for the thoughts which do not enter his head. His spirit is as great as any but its light is not brightened, the spark not fed, when he conquers the land without any dread of what he is doing. How can his soul be happy with this? How can he himself, feel at ease or be content? I am aware that in your world today, many young people take their own life. They have lost touch with that vital spark which keeps their spirit uplifted and allows natural healing to move in. Their lives are troubled with worldly things and their minds far too cluttered, for they have forgotten how to converse with their spiritual-selves. They do not seem to benefit from the natural beauty around them, for even those in your great cities could still look up and see the sky, but their eyes only look down. They miss the butterfly fluttering by and the cricket in the grass. They do not hear the birdsong. They curse the heat of the sun and yet quickly brush away the fresh raindrop which falls upon their face. The passing breeze is simply regarded as but a small relief and the four winds are of no special consequence to them . . . for their thinking is numb.

In their miserable ignorance, they believe that to take their own life is to leave behind the problems they are encountering. How terribly sad this is, for it would appear they do not realise how, when they pass into the next life, they will still need to work through the conditions which were around them here. The problems they tried to escape were important lessons being given to further progress their soul . . . lessons which cannot be ignored. In the land of Spirit, they will still need to have that experience before moving on and because it was an earthly lesson, it will be much harder for them to deal with when they are in the Spirit Realm. However, experience it, they must. I desperately want to cry out to them... "Stop! Do not extinguish yourself from this life and the chances you have been given to develop your soul." How I wish they would listen. How I wish they would nurture their own spirit while living here in the physical world.

When the spirit moves on into the next phrase of its life, the body remains on the Earthplane as an empty shell. That spark which is you carries all your thoughts and feelings with it, into the life beyond. The man who has many earthly riches is no better equipped for life in the Spirit Land, often less so, for his treasures and possessions are those which can only be of use to him in this material world. In the realms of Spirit, only if he has a richness of mind, will he be enriched. Thoughts and feelings are all you can take, they are not left behind – for indeed, they are you. Everyone has free will and may do as they wish, but all must answer to Universal Law, a law which governs everything. Maybe you do not yet believe there is a life still to come, but when you awaken in your spiritual home... and one day, awaken you will, it is to your own advantage to know where you are. But, no matter – for you will have as long as it takes. However, I would say to you... reinvigorate your life now. Feel the air around you, smell the grass and the trees. See the stars high above and enjoy all the natural things you can view, for in doing so you will refresh and uplift your spirit within.

The unnecessary taking of life is wrong, whether it be the life of a man or of a creature, or whether it be your own. Life is given by the Great Spirit and you are a part of him, for life is spirit and spirit is life. Everything that lives has a spirit... and I mean everything. Be it a mighty beast or a tiny flower, even the very earth itself, for it too lives and breathes. The world is a most beautiful place, treat it with respect. All you require is there for you to use. Mother Earth supplies all, for her healing is all around. The herbs and the flowers, the trees and the minerals, the rocks and the crystals in the ground, the food which grows on land and in water . . . all are there to nourish and sustain you, to treat your ills and keep you strong – use them well. Ask for true enlightenment to help you learn in the right way and to help others around you to also learn.

When man mistreats the animals in your world today, does he truly believe it will benefit his kind? When he farms them in such cruel conditions and causes pain and fear to fill their lives, does he really think that the right medicines will be found in this way? How can good come from so much hurt? No, my friends, nothing of lasting good can come from causing suffering to another. Animals are more sensitive than Man. Their senses are much more acute, for they are closer to Nature . . . they have not lost their natural ways. Please remember, all are living creatures, a gift from the Great Spirit. Whether they are large or small, tame or wild, they are a part of his power and therefore a part of him and consequently, a part of you. What you do to them, you do to him . . . and likewise to your own being. When you inflict pain upon them, you are storing up pain for yourself, for what you give now, one day returns to you. I have said this before – and I will say it again.

When we kill an animal, it is so we may survive and our people treat it with great respect. We also honour its spirit and send out our thanks for the renewed life it has given to us in the way of food, clothing and tools, etc. Your own 'Medicine Men' are beginning to realise that a very great number of pills and medications your people use are doing more harm than good. When you next seek a cure, ask yourself . . . "How was this made?" Did it come from the suffering of an innocent creature, for if so, all it can give in the end – is more pain. This is Natural Law. Nothing good can ever come from the deliberate act of inflicting pain upon another living thing. Ask for your own learned ones and those in a position of power to be shown the right path...the pathway which does not hurt anyone or anything, for truly peace, healing and understanding will then be returned. Think upon these words I have said, for they are indeed honest and sincere. Mother Earth can provide for all – and does.

"Just the Plea of an Indian Chief"

I seek a vision, Oh Great Spirit,
a vision clear and true,
to find the answers that I need
- to know what I must do,
this wilderness which we call home
brings beauty to our eyes,
although I fear a great unrest...
moves beneath its skies.

We love the land and rivers wide,
the mountains and the trees,
we blend within the morning mist,
we fly upon the breeze,
our heartbeat joins the rhythm
pulsating through the ground,
it's in the rock, each tiny stone...
the earth scattered around.

We are at one with all we see,
each creature we hold dear,
they are our brothers from afar,
their closeness we revere
and yet our ways are threatened,
great changes come each day,
for others move into our lives . . .
who bring with them decay.

The animals they slaughter,
the land they tear apart,
they spread disease and angry thoughts,
no truths lie in their heart,
they speak of peace, but on their terms
- our boundaries recede,
they ask to talk, but listen not . . .
our words they do not heed.

Our young are growing restless,
lack of freedom takes its toll,
they miss those open spaces
that call out to their soul,
their union with Nature,
their oneness with the Plains,
all this is now denied them . . .
their sorrow swells the rains.

Each spirit cries in anguish
and with anguish anger grows,
which brings more pain and heartache
as hatred freely flows,
revenge is not the answer
and yet all else has failed,
I'm torn within my thinking . . .
my reasoning is curtailed.

We share this world we walk in,
thus lives will be entwined
yet there is space for everyone,
no matter what his kind
and though our ways will vary
in what each may believe,
all are joined together . . .
by every breath we breathe.

I yearn for peace and harmony
to now return once more,
allowing truth and fairness
to rise up to the fore,
causing men to pause awhile,
hopefully to find
the way to live together . . .
with an open mind.

I make this plea Great Spirit,
in all sincerity,
knowing how we all must bend
just like the strongest tree,
swaying in the changes
which run throughout our lives,
but trying to keep forever . . .
the freedom of our Tribes.

22.11.02

"Just a Mistake"

Another mistake, or is it!
Perhaps it's another rung . . .
gained upon the ladder,
another song we've sung,
another step we've taken
upon life's winding way,
another lesson given –
to help us, if it may.

If we treat mistakes as lessons,
then wisdom we will earn,
for there's always a reason behind them
and from them we always can learn.
You have probably heard of the saying,
which now I would like to recall . . .
that 'The man who never made a mistake
- never made anything at all!"

We all have our hidden ideas
of the things that we'd like to see done,
but know that you really can do them
and the battle's already half won.
When and if, there appear to be problems,
then know you have made a mistake –
and with that mistake will come knowledge
of the next step that you'll need to take.

Quite often it's pride that upsets us,
it's as though we can't stand up and say
'Well, I made a mistake . . . but I'm trying
and one day I'll find the right way!'
If we never go wrong in our efforts
then how will we know when we're right,
it's the same when we can't make our minds up
- when we fail it can give us new sight.

So do not be frightened of failure
. . . it's presence will equally show
which way we were meant to follow,
the direction our pathway will go,
for life has many turnings
that we may choose to take
and often we find the right one,
by making first - a mistake!

15.8.94

CHAPTER SEVEN

Pathways

It is the beginning of our second summer together and I feel the time is right to speak to the father of Running Water and openly declare our wishes. I will approach him formally and ask if his daughter and I can be joined together as man and wife. Although we are sure he will agree to our union, it is only right to follow the custom in our village and talk with him and the Elders, requesting their joint approval and blessings. The fact we have been allowed to spend our free time with each other must show how both families are happy with the prospect of our marriage. No-one can question the love that we share – it shines from our faces and radiates around and about us, openly flowing upon the air. We have no doubts about spending our lives together. From the moment we first met, we knew we would never yearn for another. Our love is so natural, so strong and so true that we are absolutely certain it is meant to be. It would be impossible for us not to be together, for our thoughts are as one. The deep feelings we have are now so powerful that we need to unite with our bodies as well as our minds, but the respect we hold for each other helps us to resist. Our willpower is tested again and again but it remains steadfast and in a strange way, draws us ever closer to each other ... knowing how we feel and the trust we both display. Our greatest wish is to spend a healthy and contented married life together, living freely in this beautiful land where we hope to bring up our future children.

The Elders are well aware of the feelings we both share and so it is only a short time before their blessings are given. To celebrate our forthcoming union, we are invited to choose a place nearby, where we would like to set up home in our own tipi. We are thrilled about this, because it means the chosen date for our marriage will not be too far away. We have no need to ponder on where we would like to settle, for we both know immediately what our answer will be. How could we possibly choose anywhere else, except near to the waterfall where we first met. There are two other young couples in our village who are also promised to each other and everyone is agreed that we will hold the ceremonies on the last day of the Fall. We now proceed with the making of our tipi and the ever-growing friendship between the two families is clearly there for all to see.

Before these three marriages take place, the village will hold another important event. It is time for the young men who are of a similar age to myself, to find their pathway in life. This means we must spend time away, fending for ourselves . . . away from our village and from those whom we love. The idea of this is truly challenging to me and not even the thought of being separated from Running Water for a while, can dampen the excitement it brings. It is an adventure my friends and I have looked forward to for quite some time – an adventure which will decide just where we stand within our Tribe. This venture out into the wilderness is to give each one the time to learn of the person whom they really are, the person who lies deep inside – that person who is our own true self. It is a time to get to know what things we can achieve and how we can relate to our fellow men. Time to find out how well each survives, when home comforts are scarce and day-to-day living is hard. We know from then onwards, we will be leaving our youth behind as we come face to face with the changes that have to be. We all need to move forward both mentally and physically . . . but each in their own special way. Yet we must never forget those who are always close to us. Those who, if we send out our loving thoughts to them, can reach out from Spirit and touch upon our soul – those we can no longer see, but who are still there.

Although in their world time ceases to exist as we know it here on the Earthplane, life itself cannot stand still . . . it is always in motion, for nothing ever stays the same. The tiny raindrop which falls from above becomes the pool of water running into the stream. The stream flows into the river and the river gradually makes its way to the sea. The raindrop is now a part of the ocean and eventually it is drawn upwards to help form a cloud, high in the sky. Even if the raindrop remains on the ground, it is transformed into dew and becomes as a mist . . . and so the cycle carries on. Our Mother the Earth is forever changing. She does not stay the same, for her features can alter with earth-quakes and flood and the effects of the sun. The moon has its quarters and brings forth the tides and each year is governed by the seasons, which change all the time. The seed of a plant, of a creature and of woman, all evolve. The new babe grows into a child, the child becomes a youth – and the youth, a man. Just like any other seed, we develop and grow as time travels on. Life, like a circle, is never-ending.

So it is, the days and nights quickly come and go and soon it is time for my friends and I to face the challenge set before us, the challenge of leaving our youth behind . . . and taking on the role of a man. All the goodbyes have been said and the advice from our fathers rings in our ears and swims in our heads. Today is when we set off in our canoes, to move down river and so begin our journey through the wide-open spaces which lie beyond. At first we will travel together like a pack of young wolves, but without a true leader. Only when we return will we announce who that person will be and where in the pack we will all sit at ease. Although we may know of one another and seem happy in each other's company, we are at this moment, still unaware of the finer points of each individual. We may have laughed and played together when we were children, but as young adults we have not spent any serious time together. This is why we go out now as a group. We will learn not just more about ourselves but also about the characters of the others. It is hoped we will come to recognise who has the true qualities of a natural leader ... the one whom we will all be prepared to follow, when the time is right.

We will have the chance to make use of our own skills and share them with each other. Some will definitely emerge as the Peacemakers, for in any group of people, differences of opinion are bound to arise. We need to build on the casual friendship which already exists between us, so that it can develop into a lasting bond. Although problems are certain to be found, as long as we face them together and in a fair way, then we should be able to overcome them without too much time and energy being spent. There will be those who excel in hunting and the ones who are good at tracking and following a trail, yet all need to be ready to fend for themselves and so stay alive. There will be the gentle ones who are prepared to care for any who may fall ill, or spend time with those who simply need a reassuring word, or perhaps a listening ear. There will also be some whose thinking runs deeper than most – the philosophers, who delve into the reasoning behind life and can therefore help others to accept what cannot be changed. How very different people are ... and it is right that this is so, but we realise the success of a Tribe depends mainly upon the understanding and trust which exists between each one. Good leadership is important, but the beliefs and ideas of every individual, are important too.

After an unknown time, one of the Braves from our village will meet up with our group. We will then separate from the others in order to follow our own path. This will be the most difficult part, for it will mean each must live alone, drawing upon the knowledge and wisdom we have been fortunate to have received in the past. I think back to my childhood days and realise just how much I was taught, even in those tender years. Both my parents have done all they can to help me grow up safe and well and I am thankful to them. I have, of course, shared in other learning with my friends and that too, has been good. It has also been amusing for we have learnt to laugh at ourselves, as well as each other. I am glad though, that it is not just my wit which will keep me alive. Humour is a great thing and can conquer many trials, but out here we need all manner of skills to avoid danger and safely survive. We will need to watch out for the puma and the bear, as well as the snake. We know there will be a river flowing nearby and so we will be able to quench our thirst, but we must also make sure we find enough varied foods to keep our body fit and strong. Although it is the thoughts in our head which keep us alert and well protected, we must never forget how it is still the physical body which helps to feed our mind . . . each looks after the other.

I will feel quite content to be on my own for a while. To me, all this land is my home and I will have my friend the Hawk close by. I am fully aware of how I must be responsible for both myself and for his actions and that nothing can be left to mere chance. I send out a prayer for the rest of our group, that they too will find not only a strength in their thinking, but also a strength in their body as well. After the passing of one full moon, we must regroup and then travel back together to our village, here in Long Grass Creek. We stand now before our Medicine Man, as he offers up a blessing for each one, asking that all be kept safe and guided well. We hold our heads high, looking towards the sky and as I gaze into the clouds I notice my Hawk circling around – he too is anxious to be on his way. It is acceptable for him to accompany me, just as it is for the others to have their animal friends join them. It can prove to be a good safety factor, for in the case of an emergency their lone arrival back at our village would alert the Elders something was wrong.

Finally the signal is given for us to move down to the river and start on our way. With a loud whoop and a cry we run eagerly across the soft grass towards the water's edge, each one carrying within him an added determination not to fail. That determination is uppermost in our minds as we look at the swirling waters with their dancing waves. Surely, all our efforts from the previous attempts we have made to try and conquer these rapids will now come to our aid. Today, we *know* we will succeed. We slide our canoes into the clear water and skilfully jump into them, without any backward glance to those we are leaving behind. Despite our enthusiasm, we appreciate just how pensive our mothers are ... and will continue to be until we return, even though at the moment they are outwardly smiling for us, knowing how long we have awaited this day. This time out on the river, rather than battle against Mother Nature, we find the inner wisdom to relax and go with her flow. How easy it now seems. Instead of trying to feed our egos, we are happy to blend our strength with the strength of the waters upon which we ride. So it is, we are carried safely through the boulders and rocks until eventually we glide down stream, to the slower waters further along.

Compromise, instead of stubbornness! Is this not one of the secrets of life, whether living indoors or out, whether trying to survive in the wilderness or in a city, whether being alone or with others. We need the ability and the foresight not to wrestle with the elements, but to work alongside them and join with their might. Not to blindly fight against any hardships we may encounter, but to first find the reasons why they are there. When we recognise and accept the relevance of what we are faced with, then maybe the answers to problems will more readily appear and just like finding our way through the rocks in the river, we will be able to thread our way through the boulders of life. The ego is a necessary part of our being. It lifts us up and helps us to believe in ourselves, but it must always be kept under control. It should never be used against another, for it then becomes a disruptive force and can only destroy. How easy it is to let it run wild ... and once set free, it is so hard to resist the power it seems to offer. But no, my friend, it is a false understanding that it brings. Just like the rock which breaks loose from the cliff high above, it damages not only the vegetation on its fast rolling plunge, but eventually on landing, it splits into two. It may have looked dramatic and powerful as it brushed all aside, but when finally brought to a halt, it is only half of what it once use to be.

How good it is to learn from our Mother the Earth – even the rocks can teach us so much. It is like the tree which bends in the wind and so survives, or the downhill stream that takes the fastest route but in doing so, encounters more dangers. Nothing is complicated and nothing is ignored. The quivering of one blade of grass is seen by the bird and the deer in the forest hear even the faintest sound and so react. Animals are fully tuned into their way of life ... because they use all their senses to stay alert. They feel the slightest movement upon the ground and can smell the many different changes carried on the air. They listen to the knowledge deep inside them, that knowledge we regard as instinct. However, is it not simply their own spirit telling them how to behave – that inner-self which is there, concealed in each and everyone. The inner-self which we now hope to bring forth from within our own being.

We continue along the winding river, our canoes moving swiftly through the calmer waters. We feel relaxed as we enjoy the freshness of the new day and the cooling breeze, which is flowing softly over us. We look across to each other, smiling happily as we think of the many adventures that lie hidden in the journey ahead. Although we are travelling along this river, we are also travelling along another more important pathway, the pathway of life. We are again being moved forward to hopefully gain new experiences which will enrich our future outlook on who, why and what we are. Changes have to happen, even though sometimes we may try to resist them, but changes are necessary – they need to be. Without change, there could be no tomorrow and without tomorrow, we would have no new dawn and no new day. Life on Earth would cease. So it is that we now look to the changes that lie ahead.

"Just the Winds of Change"

Change is ever constant,
nothing stays the same,
only Natural Laws
can ever thus remain.
Time itself is moving,
never to be still,
seconds turn to hours
and they always will.
Space is all consuming
- no beginning and no end,
stretching out around us
its horizons meet and blend.
Yes, change is always with us,
we ride upon its flow,
at times it is so gradual . . .
we do not even know.

Feelings and emotions
are locked inside its sway,
swirling deep within us
or rising as they may.
All is ever changing
from childhood back to child,
the seasons of a lifetime
forever thus abide.
The rhythms of Eternity
are there for all to grasp –
and though they can be awesome,
they're part of life's great task.
Some changes can be sudden,
they catch us unprepared
and if at times we feel quite lost,
'tis what fate has declared.
We're tossed upon life's ocean
in seas that run so deep,
yet when the storms are greatest
. . . such treasures we can reap.
For change is so essential,
it is a natural state,
without it we could not survive –
our souls would just stagnate.
And so it is the winds of change
flutter constantly,
there to guide and carry us
to where we need to be.
Since change is never-ending,
hence it often seems
that nothing is substantial . . .
except within our dreams.

These dreams are fleeting moments
where we can rest and pause,
to seek direction, find our path
and view life's distant shores.
Such dreams of stark reality
that bid us stop and think,
are borne upon a silver thread
which keeps that vital link
- to lead us to the future,
yet hold us with the past
and help us fly on carefree winds . . .
through changes small and vast.

4.10.99

"Just Controlling the Ego"

Everyone is an individual with their own thoughts deep inside,
the good to use encouragingly, the bad to be denied
and all possess their own free will - 'tis Universal Law,
yes, come the day they judge themselves
. . . this is brought to the fore.

Everyone is different, each has his point of view
and so this is throughout the world, if to themselves they're true.
Life brings many challenges, some trivial, others great
and how we meet and deal with them
. . . our characters create.

Each person has a conscience, within their Soul it's found,
guarding them as best it can, with wisdom quite profound
and ignoring it completely will always take its toll,
for that is when their ego
. . . will rise and take control.

'Tis then true friends and loved ones can gently intervene,
reminding them they're but a stitch in life's embroidered theme.
We all have our own feelings which we can hide or share,
but if we're wise we'll always know
. . . we need to keep them fair.

No one should hurt another by unkind words or deed,
for again this is their ego which they have once more freed –
it dulls their sensitivity to what is good and right,
allowing those of lower thoughts
. . . to feed upon their light.

Ego is that weaker part which dwells within us all,
which only can grow stronger, if we heed its call,
the call of selfishness and greed, of arrogance and pride,
that tramples better feelings
. . . pushing them aside.

Quite often someone's lower self is fed by those they know,
who falsely urge them onward to feed their own ego.
Beware of not responding to your higher thoughts within
which try to point you to the light
. . . that's maybe growing dim.

You have your own opinions, borne of your own free will,
but never use another - your own dreams to fulfil,
for this will not enrich your life nor give you peace of mind,
you must make sure the good you do
. . . will truthfully unwind.

Perhaps you need more patience, perhaps the way to go
has not yet been prepared for you by those who love you so,
remember, nought comes quickly - if you're not to be misled
and knowing this may help you choose
. . . a fairer path to tread.

Controlling ones own ego is not a simple thing
for the prizes that it offers, really seem to cling,
but resisting it gets easier the more times it is done
and eventually, you will find
. . . far greater gifts are won.

28.2.02

CHAPTER EIGHT

Journey of Enlightenment

We are travelling along a stretch of the river which has low rolling hills to one side and the forest on the other. It is fairly narrow and the flow of the water is quite fast. My Hawk is high up in the sky and every so often I see him swoop downwards to vanish for a while amongst the coarse grasses, scrub or prairie sage. Two of my friends have their dogs sat with them in their canoes, while someone else has his running happily along the riverbank. It may be that this particular dog does not like the look of the rapids here, or perhaps he can remember how not so long ago, we would constantly topple over into the cold water, whenever we attempted to ride any white waves.

Dusk is falling and the rays of the sun start to drop below the far horizon. We realise we have covered quite some distance and so the decision is made to follow a shallow stream which leads off into the dense woodland. Our canoes glide gracefully between the reeds and we try to avoid disturbing the birds and creatures living there. After a short time we drag our canoes onto the grass alongside the water's edge, for everyone is of the same opinion . . . this will be a good place to spend the night. The noises from deep inside the forest are varied and we try to work out what each could be. The answers we put forward are also varied but all agree that this is definitely the kind of life we would like to lead, a life which allows us to feel in control and free. While the others go off in search of food, my friend Green

Shoots and I stay close to the canoes and make a fire. It is a beautiful evening and the air smells exceptionally fresh and vibrant. It is filled with the scent of the pine trees and makes me think yet again of being with Running Water by the falls. How great are my feelings for this young maiden and how much I miss seeing her gentle smile and lovely twinkling eyes. In this quiet moment I can almost hear our laughter floating upon the breeze.

My day-dreaming is brought to a sudden end as my Hawk flies in low over my head and lands silently upon the bough of an ancient tree, close to where I am standing. I send out a caring thought to those back home and continue with the task at hand. After gathering wood and successfully lighting a large fire, Green Shoots and I decide to indulge in a bit of harmless fun. We try catching some small fish swimming in the shallows nearby and after successfully achieving this, we quickly cook them before the others return. When our friends do reappear they find us sitting shamelessly by the fire, with three of the fish half devoured. We pretend to have eaten our fill, by leaning backwards and patting our pushed-out stomachs. This little joke is taken with good humour and brings forth a laugh. Everyone then helps in preparing and cooking the meat with which they have returned, the hunt having gone well. The food tastes good and all sleep well that first night, each taking it in turn to be on patrol. The next morning we are back on the main part of the river, which is now taking us out over the Great Plains, towards some distant hills. My Hawk is with me and he is perched quite contentedly on the rope that I have coiled up in the far end of my canoe. The river is wider here and the water deep. We have to work much harder with our paddles, for the current is running slower. The weather is changing and quite suddenly a fierce wind begins to blow. Gradually the sunshine vanishes as the sky darkens and heavy rain starts to fall.

We have now reached the far hills, which we could see from across the prairie and after a short distance the river flows into a steep-sided canyon, with caves scattered here and there. The wind has dropped but the rain is much stronger and everyone begins to feel cold and wet. It is time to seek shelter and rest. On approaching the next bend in the river, we catch sight of a group of boulders to our left and notice how the water there is very clear and the riverbed sandy. It seems a safe place to pull into with our canoes, which we leave concealed in the reeds. Gathering our few belongings, we step out onto the sand and quickly make our way to the caves seen just ahead. We then light a fire using dry grasses found growing inside the opening to one of the larger caves. It is important to settle down and eat. When the meal has ended, one of our band who is quietly looking around outside, notices footprints in a patch of damp earth. They are only just visible. We wonder if these tracks have been made by those from another Tribe . . . or are they the mark of a bare-footed white man? We realise more attention should be spent, whether in or out of our canoes, making sure we are fully aware of any who may be near. We must be more alert when first stepping ashore. These are unsettled times for those of our kind and danger could come from anywhere, at any-time. We begin to wonder if it would be wiser to move ahead. However, on reflection it is decided that because we have already been here for awhile – and because we are uncertain as to where these people may now be, it would be better to stay hidden until sunrise the next day.

We remind each other how we are out here to survive and observe, but whilst doing so we must be invisible – like the wind which travels quickly across the prairie or through the tall mountains. We must learn to hide like the puma who blends easily into the natural features of the land and . . . like the birds of prey who soar high above, we should view from afar the happenings from all around. We must be quiet like the deer, brave like the bear, as cunning as the coyote and as strong as the mighty buffalo. Yes, we have to be all of these things but most importantly, we need to tread wisely and remain unseen. While my friends are closely examining the footmarks and surrounding terrain, I suddenly catch the scent of an animal. It is easy to recognise as that of a pony and I know it must be coming from more than one. Signalling to the others to stop what they are doing, I crouch down low...and stay completely still. My friends instantly do the same. The air feels tense as we look across from one to another. Immediately, we smother our campfire with sand. All the muscles and fibres of our body are taut, our nostrils flared. Like a large cat ready to pounce, we wait and listen. The rain has almost stopped and the last of the daylight is fading fast. Three of our would-be Braves move out to search around. The rest of us divide into two groups. One group settles deeper into the dimness of the cave, while the others quietly position themselves among the rocks and foliage just outside. Carefully concealing myself between two leafy shrubs, I silently call on my spirit friends to help me stay calm. We all sense there is danger up ahead and so cover our faces and shoulders with mud made from the wet soil lying on the ground. This will help us to blend into the redness of the earth itself. The tension is almost unbearable. I finger the knife which is tied to my waist and notice others are doing the same, yet still we stay quiet...and wait.

Meanwhile, our future Braves have now found some other, clearer footprints along a narrow, isolated creek. Suddenly there is the sharp unmistakeable sound of a rifle being fired. This noise echoes wildly through the canyon, bouncing off its sheer walls and down each gully. We are unsure of what this could mean. Then, before we can even gather together our thoughts, we hear the familiar sound of ponies' hooves galloping along, followed by more gunshots. The three who have moved apart from us, immediately seek refuge in a secluded spot, hiding in dark crevices found at the base of the canyon's steep walls. It would appear others from a different Tribe have come across whitemen herding wild horses along a dry riverbed, to the east. Again there is the noise of the Whiteman's gun, this time followed by a low rumbling sound. This deep murmur increases and suddenly explodes into a noise as loud as a thunder crack, when a bolt of lightning hits the ground. Realising there has been a fall of boulders and rocks from high above, we make our way forward to find our friends. When the crimson clouds of fine choking dust begin to settle, it is a huge relief to discover that most of the wild horses had quickly scattered, thus avoiding the falling debris. However, lying almost completely buried under mounds of fallen stone, are the bodies of other horses and their white pursuers. We are aware of an eerie silence which totally engulfs all. Those from another Tribe have already disappeared. So have the rest of the Whites whom they were chasing.

As the swirling air gradually becomes clearer – and with it our thoughts – the group I am with ventures further out to continue searching for the other three. In the moonlight we see only two silhouettes. They appear to be stunned but unhurt. Soon our bleary eyes fall upon the third who is lying very still, beneath pieces of broken rock. We frantically clear them away. He is covered in blood and only half-conscious. Carefully we lie him down on the soft earth and gently cushion his head. After hurriedly lighting a fire to keep him warm and to give us more light, we cautiously feel along his limp body for any broken bones. There appear to be none and so we attend to his open wounds. He has gashes on his legs and arms, together with a deep cut on the side of his chest. Cold water from the river helps to stem the bleeding and bring him back to a more conscious state. We then carry him between us, retreating along the canyon, back to the shelter of the cave. When safely inside, his thinking slowly returns and we are pleased to find that his injuries are not as bad as we first thought. The group who remained in the cave are informed of what has taken place and they instinctively go out, to check that all is safe. They offer up a prayer for those whose lives were lost and cover with stones any of their limbs left exposed. The rest of us huddle closer to the new fire which has been made and gradually our tired bodies start to yearn for rest ... but we await the return of the our companions. Once they are back and have assured us that all is well, we post a guard and take it in turns to sleep.

It is in the early hours as the sun starts to rise, that I am gently roused from my sleep, for it is now my turn to keep watch. Before the changeover is complete, we both pause to scan the stretch of river within our view. Our instincts are right – we are not alone. Out on the water, gliding through the early morning mist, can be seen the shape of a single canoe. Quietly we wake the others. As the lone canoe draws nearer, it is quickly recognised as being one of our own and running down to the water's edge, I welcome a well-known Brave from our village. His name is Dancing Bow. After he has sat and eaten with us, we recount to him what took place the night before. He listens intently, yet without any comment, for he can tell by our serious expressions ... a most valuable lesson has already been learnt by one and all. Wishing us well, he then informs us that when we move out of the canyon later in the day, we will be greeted by another Brave who will be waiting on a grassy riverbank amongst trees, in a wooded area to the north. Our injured friend is much better and seems to have suffered no serious harm. He insists he is strong enough to continue with us. I have called upon my Spirit Healing Guides, asking for their help in keeping the wounds on his body clear from infection. Every few hours we stop, so I can carefully bathe them and waft burning sage around him.

We spend the rest of that day journeying north-west along the sparkling river, winding our way through the beauty of the deep red and amber coloured rocks which tower over us on either side of the canyon. The excitement of the previous evening has settled but the new learning it has brought, will not be forgotten. We now know we must be even more alert. Quietly dipping our paddles in and out of the shimmering turquoise water, we travel effortlessly along, our eyes constantly scanning the shoreline or horizon. At times we pause to watch the buzzards circling high above before landing in one of the many crevices, or alighting to rest boldly on a rough ledge precariously jutting out from the sheer rock face. Occasionally, after hearing the echo of small stones tumbling downwards, having being disturbed by the wild mountain goats or Big Horn sheep, we catch sight of the elusive cougar. He is stalking his prey. What an impressive creature the cougar is . . . and what a joy to see. Our minds are at peace as our spirits soar up into the blue of the sky. It is past mid-morning before anyone notices that Dancing Bow is no longer travelling with us. Just as quickly as he appeared, he has now gone. We again realise how easy it is to be too relaxed in these stunning surroundings.

Eventually the river takes us out into the grasslands and undulating hills, occasionally passing large cottonwood trees growing near to its bank. We keep a sharp lookout for the one whom we are meant to meet. Noticing more trees and shrubs in the distance, we slowly approach them and on hearing a low whistle – look across to the far embankment. There, well hidden in the thicket, crouches Tall Feathers. We dip our paddles to turn and move quietly towards him. As we draw nearer he beckons us to manoeuvre our canoes into the tall reeds and bushes, in order to hide them again. Having done this, we follow him into the woodland, where to our surprise, stands our friend Dancing Bow. How he has managed to move ahead of our canoes without anyone noticing, mystifies us all. We are delighted to find our ponies are with him. They now inform us that after today our group will split up, for each is to follow his own pathway whilst still enjoying the freedom and beauty of our homeland. It is important to make sure we avoid any kind of trouble and Tall Feathers once more reminds us that each is here to observe and learn from Mother Nature. We must also remember we are out in this wilderness to discover our own inner-selves. Everyone is to meet again at this same spot when the moon is next full and we are instructed to bring back with us something of the land – to have as a keepsake and good luck charm.

Life is like a journey...a journey which all need to travel in order to further advance their soul, just like our journey now is guiding us towards manhood. We are placed here on this Earthplane to learn and progress, for both learning and pro-gression are always there. We can enjoy them or fight against their lessons and the knowledge and wisdom they hold. We *will* make mistakes but, as we have often been told – if we are prepared to learn from them, then mistakes can be just as precious to us, as the lesson itself. However, if we simply continue to make the same mistake, then we will have gained nothing at all and the lesson will in some way, be given again. For the following weeks each one blends individually into the land and her many features. We become at one with both ourselves and the creatures who inhabit this rugged, yet wonderful terrain. We now begin to fully appreciate the help and guidance given to us by the natural elements...the sun, wind, rain, moon and stars. Even the clouds can tell us so much. We start to feel the heartbeat of Mother Earth and we sense more and more the presence of those who live in our hearts.

Our awareness of life expands . . . and so we grow. There is time out here to reflect upon the life each has known – on our infancy, childhood, adolescence and youth. We think of our families and homes and of those future families that have yet to come.

We enjoy experiencing such total freedom . . . the prairie wind blowing through our hair, the smell of fresh pine, the sweetness of the tall grasses and the fastness of our ponies, with the sound of their hooves on the rough ground underfoot. We praise the Great Spirit for the air we breathe and each breath that we take. When giving thanks for the times which are good, we now look for the good in the bad, for it has become evident to us that there is a reason for all that takes place. At times, Mother Nature can seem to be cruel – but she has to be fair to everyone and everything. When we come to accept this fact, life will feel even better and we will live more at ease with each other and ourselves. Sitting in the peace of the evening time, with the light just starting to fade and the heavens becoming streaked with red, I think again of how fortunate I am to live in such a beautiful and diverse land. From the high spiked ridges of the Black Hills to the far-sweeping Plains stretching out under a never-ending sky. From the lush green woodlands to the pink pinnacles and strange shapes of the Badlands. From the depths of a winding canyon floor to the flat top of Bear Lodge rising vertical from the prairie. From cool riverbanks to hot springs. From lofty mountains to volcanic glades. Our great Chiefs and Holymen have found many sacred places in which to sit and meditate. A great favourite is Bear Butte, where not only can they spend time on their own, but from where they can look out across this beautiful land.

The night of the full moon soon comes and one by one we return to the woodland from where we split up. All are sad to leave behind the complete freedom they have known, but are also joyful to see each other again. Our reunion is good. We spend time happily greeting one another and refreshing our ponies, who also seem pleased to be together once more. What grand tales of adventure there are to tell, but it is late ... and these stories must wait until the next day. For now, it is enough to know that each one is safe. Little Wolf, who was injured in the canyon, has completely recovered and only a slight scarring remains on one of his thighs. I thank my healing guides for their continued help.

The following evening we hold a special gathering around our small campfire to honour the Great Spirit for his guidance and protection. We think upon the discussions we have been having throughout the day, discussions concerning all the many different experiences we have encountered. We listen to those thoughts and ideas which each one has carried back in his mind and now openly shares and we once again give thanks for the learning received. Finally, we make the most important decision on who is to be our leader and what position each individual hopes to achieve. I voice my own wishes, which are to follow the ways of my grandfather and one day become our Medicine Man. Others are hoping to receive the status of a Brave while some want to work with the children and become good storytellers. As we sit in the glow of the firelight and blend in the love which radiates around, the sacred pipe is passed amongst us, for there is a great feeling of harmony, peace and true brotherhood. One of the hopeful new Braves, Red Flame, has been chosen to be our group leader ... and it is to him we now turn. The rest of the night is spent in dance and in song and we create a makeshift drum, making sure its sound will not resonate too loud.

The next morning finds us again joined by Tall Feathers and Dancing Bow, who in turn, warmly congratulate Red Flame on his achievement. Then, after we have settled ourselves into our canoes, they quickly ride off, leading the ponies safely home. We watch as they gallop away, one at the front of our trusted steeds and the other bringing up the rear. As our canoes float out into the middle of the river, it is Red Flame who guides us on our way and everybody feels happy with the decision we have made. He is a fine young man, one who can be trusted and respected. He has a noble, yet humble air and everyone feels proud to have him as the leader of our group. On arriving back in the familiar stretch of the river approaching our village, we climb out of the canoes to wait patiently for Tall Feathers and Dancing Bow. When they again appear with our ponies, we ride with them towards our tipis, the smoke of which can now be seen. Red Flame is at the front of the line, together with Tall Feathers and Dancing Bow on either side of him.

What a great feeling it is, for the whole village has turned out to witness our return. We are met first by the Elders in their full tribal dress and then by our families, who are moving up from a little way behind. Following them are the children who jump up and down, waving their little hands and shouting loudly. It is a day I shall never forget. As soon as the formalities have ended, I hug both my mother and father, before striding proudly over to Running Water. Oh how I have longed to hold her. We stand together, locked in each other's arms, just so happy to enjoy the nearness of the other's body. I smell the sweetness of her hair and rejoice in the thought that this is the young woman who will soon become my wife. I continue to hold her close, for she is so much a part of me – indeed we truly live in each other's heart. I send out a silent prayer that she may always walk by my side and that one day she will become the mother of my children. My whole being aches for her as I slowly relax in the softness of our warm embrace. Yes . . . this is the woman for whom I live.

Running Water also senses the harmonious energies which are swirling about them. She is both happy and grateful to again have Two Wings beside her and she feels such joy as he draws her to him. Suddenly, it is as though they have never been apart. She can feel his strong arms around her as she presses her body gently against his and she knows without question, that she will always be safe when he is near. It is difficult for them to believe how much they have each missed the other's presence. Running Water looks lovingly up into the eyes of Two Wings, as he tenderly strokes her hair. At the same moment Morning Mist runs over towards them, for she too wants to welcome him home. She excitedly explains how those who stayed behind in the village have prepared an evening of song and praise . . . to mark their safe return to Long Grass Creek.

As the night and its shadows close in, Running Water and I walk hand in hand to our own special place by the waterfall. There we laugh and kiss together in the moonlight, as tears of pure happiness glisten on our faces. Opening the small bag I have carried over my shoulder, I show her the keepsake brought home from my travels. It is quite an unusual stone with various colours running through it – one which I found amongst tall reeds growing in a dried-up riverbed, when I wandered through yet another steep-sided canyon. She gasps, exclaiming how beautiful it is . . . and then her eyes sparkle even brighter as I place in her palm a second one, almost identical to the first. This other stone I have brought home for her. She cradles it in her hands as we continue to smile at each other.

While we were away, it appears that the distant troubles with the Whiteman have increased and sadly, even larger numbers of them are taking over the land. There have been many small battles fought . . . and lost by both sides. Even greater losses have occurred of men, women and children. We wonder how it will end. There seems to be an immense change coming for those of our kind, one which carries a sense of foreboding. We note there is a strange restlessness in the air which does not feel right. It is something which we cannot define – and the future lies uncertain in our minds.

>>>> <<<<

"Just Memories of the North American Indian"

Across the vast prairie where the
eagle likes to soar,
from home to home, I love to roam
. . . its beauty to explore.

Out on the open grasslands, my
companions by my side,
beneath the sky, with head held high
. . . upon the wind I ride.

Deep in the mighty canyons with
their rivers constant roar,
the colours glow, the waters flow
. . . I quietly stand in awe.

Through the majestic Black Hills, their
valleys deep and wide,
I feel the peace, my worries cease
. . . my heart is filled with pride.

Far out upon the Great Plains where
our fathers dwelt before,
I find myself, that inner wealth
. . . which speaks of Spirit Law.

Within the quiet woodlands among
the trees I stride,
there healing's found, from all around
. . . and spirit does abide.

Beyond this time, through sacred dreams,
I truly know for sure,
the buffalo herds, in other worlds
. . . drift on forever more.

29.7.01

"Just Sitting Round the Campfire"

I hear within the campfire's song
lost wisdom echoing along,
it floats across the distant hills,
o'er plains and woodlands, streams and rills.

I see within the campfire's flame
past images arise again,
they dance until they thus become –
the rhythm of the reed and drum.

I smell within the campfire's smoke
the sweet aroma of the oak,
the slender elm, the ash and beech,
the yew and pine . . . my senses reach.

I feel within the campfire's glow
the touch of those I used to know,
they're in the breeze, the sun and moon,
the rain and snow, the whirlwind's plume.

I hold within the campfire's heat
the river's flow, the snake's heartbeat,
tumble and bindweed, herbs and seeds,
pony and eagle, coloured beads.

I watch within the campfire's light
strong thoughts arise into the night,
those healing rays that spread out wide
from burning embers . . . purified.

I find within the campfire's ring
a sense of me - I want to sing.
I share the peace and thus embrace
the memories of a wiser race.

I sit within the campfire's sphere
and join with those who now appear,
we blend in love and harmony
on yonder plain . . . our spirits free.

15.12.97

"Just Stories from the Great Plains
. . . Bear Butte"

The Great Spirit is with me, I feel this inside,
yet never so more - than when here I abide,
for on this sacred ground, no truths are denied.

Silver Birch trees are swaying and birds join in song,
while the smell of the pine drifts sweetly along,
refreshing my mind, keeping it strong.

The most gentle of breezes caresses my face,
touching my heart as its presence I trace,
for these are passed loved ones, who send their embrace.

In this special moment, with others I stand,
the ones who walked with me in this rugged land,
who nurtured my being . . . led me by the hand.

I love them so dearly, they speak to me clear,
I raise up my senses to help them draw near -
they know my intentions are always sincere.

As they send me fresh hope with guidance anew,
I relax in the healing also sent through
and wrapped in their love, dissolve into the view.

Down through the woodland my thoughts I now send,
towards the Great Plains where our destiny blends
with Tatanka, the Buffalo . . . the most loyal of friends.

These places I'm drawn to are precious to me
- the Black Hills, the Badlands, the open prairie.
When to them I venture, my spirit flies free.

Bear Butte, Mato Paha, calls out to my Soul
for back in the past, it played a great role . . .
being here makes me happy, it makes me feel whole.

27.4.10

CHAPTER NINE

Life Moves On

As the summer months pass and we move into the season of change known as the Fall, so the time for our marriage draws near. The many shades of green in the forest gradually begin to fade and the beautiful rustic colours start to appear. This autumn brings not only a change in nature, but also a change in the lives of Running Water and myself. High above the tree-tops, we can once again hear the geese flying close together on the wing and this makes me think how uplifting it will be to have my sweetheart close to me. The fresh breezes are now cooler and evening comes much quicker, but no matter how bad the weather may turn or how stormy it may be . . . I know we will always have each other's love to keep us strong.

The morning of our special day dawns and there is great excitement in the village. The families involved are busy preparing for the grand celebrations which will take place after the wedding ceremony itself. The three young brides are being pampered and adorned with pretty flowers and are indeed the centre of attention – and quite rightly so! There is a noticeable coming and going, for the whole community is filled with an air of joyful anticipation. I and the other two bridegrooms are also receiving plenty of attention before being decorated with prairie sage and colourful braids. Running Water looks quite delightful and I feel so proud, knowing soon we will become man and wife.

The noon ceremony takes place in the Lodge of the Elders and involves a beautiful exchanging of words. As people finally settle into their places, the smaller children continue playing outside, their gentle laughter carried on the breeze. Its sound adds to the happiness flowing all around. Everyone listens intently to the promises being made and though the words may be simple – their meanings are most sincere. Tears of emotion can be seen in the eyes of the older women, who are quietly recalling their own special memories. As a visible token of our undying love, small personal gifts are exchanged between each bride and groom, one to the other. After this, everyone makes their way to a huge campfire which gives out a warm glow in the softly fading light. Great rejoicing can now be heard as the drum beat and the women's tremolo (a vibrating sound without words) signals the festivities to start. The newly-wed couples invite the children of the village to join in and so they dance around, in their own enchanting way. Next, the Braves put on a most energetic and powerful display as the beating of the drum becomes faster and faster. Eventually it is the turn of the women and girls, who sing sweetly and gently sway. The parents of each bride and groom are congratulated by the Elders and a magnificent feast is served, to be enjoyed by everyone. It has been a grand occasion, one Running Water knows she will never forget. She glances across to her sister Morning Mist, hoping that when the time is right, she too will find someone sincere . . . to love and care for her.

The day is drawing to a close and I notice Running Water is looking coyly over to her grandmother, who smiles back at her, before nodding affectionately. My shy young bride then turns and takes hold of my hand. Beneath the fullness of the moon with the twinkling stars lighting up the darkened sky, we joyfully make our way to our own tipi, amidst harmless shouts of encouragement from friends of our age. That night, our love is finally sealed and we know for certain ... for the rest of our lives *and* in the lives beyond, we will never want to be too far away from each other. Our togetherness is complete and our hearts truly sing.

While the leaves on the trees turn to red, orange and gold, so the leaves in the book of life continually change with the passing of time. The snows softly fall and Running Water and I spend the bitterly cold winter locked away in our own little world, almost oblivious to life outside. What wisdom the Elders showed in suggesting the end of the Fall for our union to take place. What better season to retreat from it all. It is a time just for us. Though the springtime will indeed be no quicker in coming than she has been in any other year, I cannot help thinking how it seems to be the shortest winter I've ever experienced, such is our love and our complete indifference to the wet and freezing weather. The seasons move on . . . through the hazy summer months to the crisp, cool days that quickly follow, until winter-time again gives way to spring – and another hot summer. Then, in the last days before autumn, as the wild flowers continue to bloom, Running Water becomes aware of the new life growing inside her. How delighted everyone is and what joy it brings. As my young wife gains weight, the women realise that because of her size, this is going to be a double birth. Now there is even more excitement! I am just relieved our babies will enter this world in the warmth of the late spring.

The wars with the Whiteman intensify. One morning just after sunrise, while riding out on the open prairie with my friends, our attention is drawn to a most unusual odour which is flowing intermittently upon the air. There are six of us, four being Braves. It is our intention to race our ponies across the distant Plains, but we are completely unaware of what this strange smell could mean and decide there and then – we need to know. By following this odorous trail, it leads us to the furthermost point of our tribal domain, for we are heading now towards the foothills of another mountain range over in the west, those known as the Big Horn Mountains. Before reaching them, we veer off northwards along the Greasy Grass River, in a valley the Whites call the Little Big Horn. As dusk falls, we ride to the highest ridge of some undulating hills and from there look down on a most devastating scene. Our horses start to behave in a very distressed way, for here the nauseating smell is so acute, it is almost unbearable. Finally, its source becomes clear. Spreading out before us lies the evidence of a most terrible battle, with both animal and human remains littering the blood-stained earth. We find it hard to believe what our eyes are seeing. It is a sight none of us shall ever forget. Scattered everywhere are broken Indian lances and military swords, left standing upright but at varying angles from the ground – and among the green buttes and rippling grasses, stands a long pole. Hanging from it and fluttering pathetically in the wind, are the shredded remains of an American flag. It is obvious that hand-to-hand fighting has taken place amongst the small hillocks and ravines surrounding us.

We ask each other – "How can such a thing happen? How can there be such a waste of life? How can life become so cheap? Where is the reasoning and what is the reward?" To us it makes no sense at all! How can any man justify what we have seen? Life is a gift from the Great Spirit and this gift should never be abused. Why . . . even the smallest of creatures is precious and should never be maimed nor wantonly hurt. Surely it would be much better for men to talk with one another and come to terms with their differences, for here – there was nought. What we did not know was that many of our Chiefs were constantly striving to make peace, but with no lasting success. Our horses are very restless and we fear we are ill-equipped to defend ourselves against any group of armed soldiers who may be near, for it is evident this battle has not long been fought. Turning around, we begin our journey back to Long Grass Creek and realise we have travelled much further than we thought. We'd left just after dawn and were now well outside our usual territory. It is not wise to be unprepared when venturing so far afield. Riding homeward across the prairie, we continue to wonder how men can be led into this kind of war. The land is vast and within reason – there is enough for all.

In the early hours of the next morning we arrive back at our village and with great sadness, report to the Elders what we had found. After listening intently to our words, they express their deep concern – not just for what we had seen, but for our travelling so far away without their knowledge. Though they understand why we followed the trail, we are still reprimanded for not being more cautious. Riding out there without any prior preparations having been made to secure our safety, was not good! Of course, they are right. However, as young men, we are only just beginning to grasp the full extent to which our lives are being changed. The six of us feel rather solemn for the next few weeks. We have sadly come to realise just how right our friends the Cheyenne were, when they felt so dejected about the white soldiers they had seen, moving in from the east.

Whilst we were away, an unusual incident occurred in our village concerning a young Brave. He had been at the river's edge when the Great Bear suddenly lunged out of the forest and across one of the streams. Although the dogs did try to stop her, she came dangerously close to a small child. It turned out to be a mother grizzly with her infant cub. The young Brave was Blazing Bow. He had instinctively run forward and placed himself in front of the terrified youngster, who in sheer panic had tripped and fallen. Fortunately, during all the noise and confusion, the cub became disorientated and ran off in the opposite direction. Before following her fleeing offspring, the huge bear lashed wildly out at Blazing Bow and with one mighty strike, almost severed his left arm. As others rushed to his aid, the bear turned to look for her frightened cub, who was retreating deeper into the forest. Mercifully, because of her motherly concern, she followed her little cub and quickly disappeared amongst the dense foliage and broken tree trunks. After comforting the child, Blazing Bow was carried to my Grandfather's lodge.

Over the following weeks, the natural healing potions and skills of our Medicine Man, together with caring thoughts, save the life of the young Brave – but nothing can be done to fully restore the use of his arm. He does not take it well. The healing of his mind is much harder to achieve, for it has to come from his own spirit within. He is angry and confused and Grandfather decides to take him under his wing. For four consecutive days he leads Blazing Bow out onto the Great Plains where he can vent his anger and try to come to terms with his fate. Very gradually, his hurt starts to ease as he learns to accept what has taken place. He begins to realise that perhaps the loss of one arm is a small price to pay for gaining the life of a child . . . for indeed, without his bravery, the child would not have survived.

Blazing Bow now understands how a great honour has been bestowed upon him, for truly, nobody can question that he has fully earned the title of – 'Brave'. A special meeting around the campfire is arranged, to show the great respect everyone holds for him. Since facing up to the consequences of what occurred, he is ready to continue his life in the best way he can . . . and this he does. All his previous thinking had been submerged in the anger felt for what happened to him, but once Blazing Bow accepted the price he'd had to pay, his right thinking returned and he became a much happier man. Acceptance of a situation does not take that situation away, but it does make it easier to endure. Here is yet another lesson for all to share.

As time passes, the months come and slowly go, until one warm day the snows of winter begin to melt, for springtime is returning. The trees regain their leaves and early blossoms appear. Eventually, more and more green shoots and coloured flowers push their way through the moist earth. The heat of the sun increases the activity both in the village and in the woodland. Bird and animal alike rear their young. So it is, the birth of my own two children falls due. The women are busily attending to Running Water and our Medicine Man is near to hand. I sit nervously with my friends, eagerly awaiting news. When it comes, it is not from one of the women . . . but from the cries of the newborn. I rush to the side of my love and cradle her face in my trembling hands. Then I see the two babes she now tenderly holds. These are our children, so small and so new. Surges of emotion sweep over me as I hear my mother whisper . . . "You have a girl and a boy." It is hard to catch my breath, for what elation I feel. My mother tells me all has gone well and that Running Water is strong and has not lost too much blood. Our babies are tiny, but oh – what a joy! Gently they are lifted up and placed in my arms. Nestling them safely against my chest I feel overwhelmed with love. I smile down at their mother, who is almost asleep. Mindful of the two precious bundles I am holding, very carefully I kneel beside her and entwined in the magic of this memorable moment, we all share in a long and loving embrace. We stay like this, joined together in our happy and contented thoughts, until the light fades and ends the day. The Great Spirit has truly blessed us with the most sacred of gifts.

The weeks turn into months and the year passes away. As our children grow, so does the love continue to grow between their mother and myself. It is now over a year and a half since our family increased and I sit happily watching my two youngsters playing together in the short grass, around our tipi. Our life is good here, at Long Grass Creek. We have named our son 'Two Feathers' and our daughter 'Dancing Stream'. I think on how innocent and beautiful they look, both gurgling and laughing in the sunshine. It makes me feel proud that even at this tender age, Two Feathers is so protective and helpful to his twin sister. I glance across at Running Water who is preparing our meal... and just for a moment, catch an air of sadness around her, a sadness which I'd noticed briefly two days before. I had wondered then, what it could be, but with the children becoming more active, I'd decided she was probably tired. At that time, I felt there was no need to be unduly concerned – but how wrong my thoughts would turn out to be.

It is a few hours later, when Grandfather approaches and asks if I will accompany him to his lodge, for he wishes to talk with me. Immediately, I know by his sombre face that he is troubled within. It is a warm, scented evening, but I am only aware of an uneasiness inside me, as we walk silently side by side back to his tipi. Once there, he hesitates for a moment – and then bids me enter. I do so and we both sit down to smoke the sacred pipe. After a long pause he slowly speaks. He enquires if there is anything worrying me? I answer that all is well... and then recall the few times I'd sensed an unusual quietness with Running Water, a quietness which I had queried, but not really pursued. Suddenly I begin to feel very unsure. Maybe I should have done more to find out the reason for it. Grandfather then asks about our children. Again, I reply how all is fine. With great sensitivity, my grandfather relates to me how he has noticed a slowness around Dancing Stream, which does not seem right. He tells me Running Water has confided to him, her concern. Not wanting to unduly upset me – and taking into account that he is our Medicine Man, she had sought his advice. Feeling a panic building up in my gut, I quickly mumble, "Maybe it's simply that Two Feathers is developing faster than his sister!"

However, inwardly I know it is usually the other way around. Usually, the girl-child would be the quicker to learn. Grandfather makes no further comment . . . he has said what he needed to.

As precious time passes and our children grow older, the slowness of Dancing Stream becomes more noticeable. I sit and watch and listen, trying hard to take it in. Perhaps there is a hidden reason why Two Feathers is so protective of her. Perhaps he knows . . . what we are yet to discover. Now it has been brought to my attention, I sadly begin to realise how Dancing Stream does not react as readily as she should. Yet she appears to be such a contented and happy child. There is much I need to learn. During the autumn months it becomes more and more obvious our young daughter is not responding as I had first thought. Yes, there is something definitely wrong. My grandmother is the one who helps me to understand. She explains how Dancing Stream, although happy – is slow in her mind. A great heaviness falls upon me and I feel my head swimming in disbelief. How can this be and what can I do? Surely there will be potions to help her. What about the medicines Grandfather uses and the healing which can filter through? What about the prayers we can all send out? These questions spill over as I struggle to think more clearly.

Grandmother very gently takes my arm. "Two Wings," she says, "you must be strong. Your little one is not suffering in *any* way. She is joyful and contented. The things she has not learnt . . . and never will, are of no loss to her, for she does not even know they exist. In her own reasoning, all is well, because she does not hurt. The hurt is borne by those who are only aware of what they consider she will miss. Know that her pathway will be free from the heartache and pain most people experience as they develop and grow. Nothing can take away her happy outlook – because that innocence we have as a child, will remain with

109

her throughout her life. Remember how we are taught that sometimes we come to this Earth, not to learn lessons... but with lessons to give. It would appear Dancing Stream has come with lessons for us all. Together we will learn, but first we must accept what needs to be."

That night, I hold Running Water much closer to me and whisper to her, how all will be well. Our little family will cope with this and be happy. Two Feathers, just like my own twin, will have enough strength for both of them. Our extra concern will bind us all that bit closer and our lives will continue to be good. Nought has changed except that our understanding of life has had to increase. We are still a loving family. We still have our dear children... and we will always have each other. I suddenly begin to realise how life teaches us in ways we least expect and sometimes those ways prove to be extremely difficult. As a Medicine Man, my grandfather has been put into a situation where his natural potions and medicines cannot cure his great grand-daughter. However, he knows his healing thoughts will be of immense benefit, for who can say – without them, maybe Dancing Stream would not survive. Running Water and I have the two children we so wanted, but we have had to accept a responsibility which is much more than we could previously have imagined. Acceptance is definitely the answer, just like it was for Blazing Bow when he lost the use of his arm, those many years ago. Acceptance and the determination to make the most of a situation, is truly the key to finding contentment. No... acceptance does *not* take the situation away, but it certainly helps to ease the sadness which can otherwise linger. So it is that life goes on – the years pass and I become an older and wiser man.

>>>> <<<<

"Just a Tender Love"

Love is sharing, love is caring, love is here with you today,
bringing laughter, ever after . . .
in sweet memories to stay.

Love is showing, love is flowing, love is trying, come what may,
growing bolder, as we're older . . .
finding strength along life's way.

Love is learning, love is burning, love is keeping hurt at bay,
gaining healing, by revealing . . .
inner feelings, less they stray.

Love is sacred, love is naked, love is truth freed from decay,
shining brightly, blending quietly . . .
in our work and in our play.

Love is caring, love is sharing, love is knowing what to say,
offering kindness, ever timeless . . .
held within love's golden ray.

7.5.99

"Just Gaining Experience"

How dare we say we understand . . . without
experience, gained first-hand.

How cruel we feel this life to be
when things go wrong for you and me
and yet we know there is a plan,
which covers every single man
- a plan that's ruled by Spirit Law
and not what we are asking for.
We're here to learn within this life,
to sample good . . . to sample strife,
for without both how could we know
just how differently they flow.
Could we say the sun is bright
if we had never seen the night?
Can we appreciate our gain
if we do not know of pain?
In others heartaches can I share
unless I too, have needed care?
'Til I experience what I see –
it does not mean the same to me!

I must accept I need to know
the traumas that beset me so
and in this knowing seek and find,
the answers which bring peace of mind,
not only for ourselves but those
whose sad concern quite clearly shows.
The lessons which around us twine
may also help their light to shine.
Our suffering can bring insight
for those trapped in a similar plight.
Receive life's problems as a gift
that test the mind, the soul uplift,
for in our struggle there's a cause,
decreed by Universal Laws.
True wisdom gained along this way,
is locked within and will not stray
and with such knowledge we then earn –
the right to help others to learn.

How dare we say we understand . . . without
experience, gained first-hand.

18.4.96

"Just the Circle of Life"

Life moves in circles, spiralling round,
when we understand that . . . understanding is found.

Life is unending, nothing can cease,
if this is accepted . . . we'll gain inner peace.

Life is a puzzle, from which we may learn,
while this is acknowledged . . . then knowledge is earned.

Life is so precious, it does not stop here,
once this fact is realised . . . each path seems more clear.

Life is eternal, our spirit divine,
when this is remembered . . . much brighter we shine.

22.11.00

CHAPTER TEN

The Badlands . . . Mako Sica

As the sun starts to drop below the horizon and the sky turns to a fiery red, I am standing with my young son Two Feathers, looking at the tall pinnacles which rise up along the narrow pathway, stretching out ahead. Their red, pink, orange and yellow bands of colours are enhanced in the fading daylight and soft shadows play tricks upon our tired eyes, but what intense beauty before us lies. We are travelling through Mako Sica, the Badlands of South Dakota, a most dramatic and magical landscape, steeped in grace. With its extreme shapes and unusual rock formations, it brings forth a spiritual awareness . . . and a strange sense of having been there before. We both stand in awe. The stillness of the moment is suddenly disturbed by the piercing call of a large solitary bird of prey, swooping directly over our heads. It seems to have appeared from nowhere and flies even lower as it moves away along a narrow dried-up riverbed. What energy is in those powerful wings. We wonder if it will circle around before reappearing. This is a prairie falcon and its lone haunting cry blends in well with these mysterious surroundings.

Our loyal ponies have carried us safely along the uneven track which meanders slowly upwards from the Grasslands and Great Plains, stretching out now far behind. We watch as the last of the light begins to fade, the clouds bathed in a crimson glow. We will spend the night out here beneath the stars, in this wild domain . . . and what beauty will be ours. What a wonderful experience for my son. Such joy it brings into my heart. It is a time for further learning, a time for new and interesting things. I smile to him and immediately my smile is returned with a cheeky, yet innocent grin – but the hour is getting late and tomorrow we must make an early start. We collect dry grasses and other materials to light a fire, which, through the approaching darkness, will provide the warmth and protection we need.

Although Mako Sica may at first appear to be quite empty of life, there are many creatures who make it their home. Out here, members of the Great Spirit's family are able to wander freely. This is a wilderness where past and present can truly be found. Here, we are shown how everything is connected – from the low rolling prairie, to the tops of the buttes whose remnants of the higher prairie are still grassy and green . . . from the many different coloured layers in the sheer rock faces, to the nodules of clay lying at ground level, around their base . . . from today's living animals and birds, to the many fossils hidden in the stones. An amazing variation of colourful hues from the mixed grasses, flowers, plants and cacti, are also drawn to the eye.

We gather more grass to prepare a bed for the night, near to the stones around the fire which is burning brightly as its flames merrily leap and dance. The quick-changing weather out on the Great Plains is very unpredictable and the still, gentle air can suddenly be replaced by a fierce storm. Our thick buffalo robes will be wrapped firmly around us while we sleep, for it is important we stay dry and warm. Before settling down we shall eat some of our pemmican. This is dried buffalo meat which has been pounded into a paste and mixed with wild berries and buffalo fat. It is very tasty and certainly good to eat. We will also drink a small amount of the water we have carried with us . . . but first we must attend to our horses. As the stars begin to sparkle in the night sky and we settle down next to one another upon the sweet smelling grasses, we hear a movement on the rough stones behind us. Perhaps it is a prairie dog and if so, it is more than likely there are black-footed ferrets also running around. Then without any warning, a dark shape passes by, flying very low. This is a night hawk and from across the long grass we hear a muffled squawk. The scuffling noise we heard on the stones abruptly stops and I now know it must have been made by a chipmunk, who has undoubtedly become the night hawk's prey. Two Feathers turns towards me with an anxious expression on his little face, but I gently calm and re-assure him, for he must understand how this is Nature . . . this is her way.

The time has come to sleep. Before doing so we sit for a short moment, gazing into the flames flickering in the fire. The darkness around us is once more quiet. I let my mind drift and think of days long gone and of my Ancestors. They too enjoyed riding out here to spend time in the open, absorbing the peace and solitude. I am in a happy, but pensive mood, for although the different seasons come and go, memories last forever. Beneath the moon and the thousands of twinkling stars, my son falls fast asleep beside me, as I play a soft lilting tune upon my flute. I think about his mother, for he is still only young and tonight is the first time he has been so far away from her. I am certain she will be feeling concern for him, but soon he will grow and need to be free. Lessons learnt now will remain forever and experiences like this are precious, for they always bring with them such wisdom. I stare up at the heavens, just like I did as a boy and remember my own parents who showed such caring and love. This makes me realise how fortunate I have been. I must nurture my two children as much as possible, for childhood is short and life can be long and hard. Learning through love can help keep one strong. The notes from my sacred flute gently float upwards and as I continue playing, I imagine them travelling out across the prairie to our tipi back home in Long Grass Creek. I send out more loving thoughts to my wife. Although it was only yesterday morning when we left, I am already wishing she were here beside me. I start to visualise Dancing Stream, our little daughter, and wonder if she is missing her brother. My mind relaxes in the love we as a family share, until my day-dreaming fades into tiredness and sleep. In prayer I have asked the Great Spirit to hold us all safe within his keep.

As the dawn starts to show I look across at our first-born, who is not yet awake . . . then I rise and check our ponies. All is fine. Gathering some of the prairie sage, I slowly breathe in its aromatic smell. My son eventually begins to stir. His eyes blink as his little arms stretch out and his lungs take in the goodness of the fresh morning air. As I watch him, he promptly sits up and with wide-open eyes, shuffles across to sit with me. Together we eat more of our food before drinking sparingly from our water bag. There are freshwater springs here, but only a few. I feel we should leave their water for those creatures who have hardly any, for without these springs they could have none. I take time to explain this to Two Feathers, for I want him to learn that the water is there for all to share.

Suddenly three small pronghorns run swiftly across the bare open ground in front of us, disturbing a bird who promptly panics and takes to the sky. Throughout the Badlands there are a variety of animals and I admire them all for the ways in which they manage to survive – it takes a special kind of determination to stay alive out here. I always look forward to seeing a coyote or maybe a wolf, though my special thoughts are forever with our friend, the mighty buffalo. There are also white-tailed deer, bighorn sheep, mule deer, foxes, badgers, porcupines, the nocturnal toads and many others. All these, we regard as part of our natural family and of course, I must not fail to mention the cottontail rabbits whom our children adore. As well as the many four-footed creatures, we find different coloured moths and butterflies, grouse, songbirds, owls and other birds of prey. One of the most dangerous yet exciting of creatures is the rattlesnake. Our horses are very quick to respond if we hear the unmistakeable sound he can make. The noise of his rattle is all it takes to warn us he is close, although before hearing that, we would hopefully have already picked up on our horses' fear. Our young people need to know how to be aware of such dangers, so they may learn how to avoid them and though experience can be a hard teacher, it is still one of the best *and* a good form of defence.

The new day has now dawned and it is time to kneel upon Mother Earth, who has been warmed by the strong rays of the sun. We welcome the daylight into our world and we honour the four winds and the freshness they bring. I help Two Feathers light some sage and he wafts it around as we remain kneeling side by side. The burning of prairie sage is a healing rite and with my open hands I draw its fragrant smoke towards and around us both. This 'smudging' will help my little son to cope with the rest of our journey. As we stand up he again smiles at me. The sky is turning a lovely blue. Taking the reins of my horse I lead it across the loose shale towards the main track. My son is quick to copy whatever I do. Together we walk along with our ponies before mounting and riding uphill for a while, until we are high above the open plains. I glance at Two Feathers . . . and yes, everything I do, he tries to do the same. It was so with myself and my own father and thus with his father before him. What better way is there to learn? I know one day in the far-off future, my boy will also teach his son – and so the learning will continue.

Slowly we succeed in reaching the top of Sheep Mountain Table and the view is quite breathtaking. From up here we can see large areas of gullies, cut so deep that even the wild goats find them difficult to negotiate. Scattered around are the flat tops of buttes covered in grass, making them look like green islands marooned in a sea of rock. It has been an arduous climb to the top, but it is certainly well worth the effort. My young son is jubilant, even though his little legs are aching, for in the steeper parts we had to walk instead of ride. The Badlands are indeed magnificent. They are like no other place I have ever seen. They give one the feeling of having stepped into a dream-world. I am so pleased Two Feathers is here with me.

After one more night camped on the flat summit, the time has sadly come to leave. It will be good to return to my wife and daughter – and Two Feathers is now becoming restless to see his mother again. He has also missed his twin sister. As we turn our horses around to begin the long journey home, I ponder on what these past few days have meant to us both. For myself, it has offered me the time to refresh my spirit and also to let my fatherly love unroll . . . a chance, while I am still young, to relate in a man's own way to his little son, whose real journey through life is only at its beginning. For Two Feathers, I hope his time out here has been enjoyable. I hope there have been lessons learned which he will come to respect, lessons that when he is older, he will put to good use.

Moving downwards, we start to lose the cooler air from high above and the heat becomes severe. For a while we shelter from the sun inside the opening to a shallow cave, where we quench our thirst. Close by are tiny chipmunks running around rocks and along a dry creek. Two Feathers laughs out loud when he hears them squeaking to each other and when one stands still, he cannot resist moving towards it . . . but in an instant, they are gone. I help him back onto his pony and we press on with our descent. The long climb down is past its worst and all at once, we find ourselves riding amongst a mixture of colours, for small sunflowers of yellow, orange and beige, mirror the similar colours running through the rocks. Gradually we start to leave behind the narrow canyons and high peaks of the Badlands, as the path becomes almost level. Out here, the features of the land are more green than brown and there is a slight breeze blowing. On approaching a large prairie dog town, we both turn to each other and immediately start smiling. Although prairie dogs are plump they *are* agile and here they are busy chasing each other around, having just emerged from beneath the ground. Some criss-cross the stubby grassland while others cautiously peep out from the entranceways to their burrows. They are very sociable animals with a clear high-pitched bark and they frequently call out to their nearest neighbour, lifting up their cute faces in a variety of comical poses. Their habit of balancing themselves upright on their short back legs always amuses Two Feathers. We pause to watch them suddenly popping up here and there, until it is time for us to venture further on.

The sight of the many different flowers and grasses together with the colourful cacti blooms and the gnarled old juniper trees, is very uplifting and it pleases me how my son shows an interest in all that is around him. I draw his attention to the Poison Ivy plant, whose three-pointed leaves and lack of thorns make it quite easy to recognise. We are now moving through the grasslands to the Great Plains beyond . . . and all is well. Sitting contentedly on my horse's back, I feel so proud watching my four-year-old boy riding with such ease. He too, is relaxed and happy. Since before he could even crawl, in fact almost from when he was born, he has known the different rhythms of a horse beneath him and the many varying sounds made by its hooves upon Mother Earth. His ability to ride is extremely good, for he is Lakota – and it flows in his blood. He has been taught to respect his pony and to help care for it in the correct way. His grandfather often says – "He will one day become a great horseman." I quicken the pace knowing how eager he is to race with me. We have now moved further out, onto the open prairie. Our horses are of a good breed and with nostrils flared, they very quickly increase their speed. Faster and faster we both ride. Two Feathers is clearly enjoying himself, although I am not sure what his mother would think. Eventually I let him pass me and as his horse overtakes mine, he raises one hand in an unmistakeable gesture of glee. Now, for a brief moment it is I who am uncertain, for he has never ridden this fast before. We both change to a trot and continue at a more reasonable pace. He gives a large grin which stretches from ear to ear and I in return, put a pained expression upon my face. This makes him laugh out yet again.

Today is exceedingly hot. We are making our way towards a wide river with its soothing waters. In my thoughts I offer my humble thanks we have come to no harm and that here, we can fully quench our thirst. While our horses drink from the shallows, we dismount and chant a song of praise in true acknowledgement of Mother Nature's beauty, knowing it is right that we do. Then we also drink, before teasingly chasing each other around, splashing about in the river's cold but refreshing flow. Our hearts sing for we feel so privileged to have felt the presence of the Great Spirit, Wakan Tanka out here, in this wild and remote landscape. In the Badlands we have experienced his great might in the rocks, stones, creeks and canyons, as well as the tall buttresses. We have enjoyed the company of his creatures and taken delight in the many flowers and beautiful colours. We thank him sincerely for giving us these earthly treasures.

As we remount to continue our journey home, I quietly take a look back at Mako Sica and hope we will soon be able to return.

Here there is so much to learn...not just of Nature, but of one's own self. I shall miss being in its awesome presence, which helps me to find a deeper, inner wealth. My son, though still only young, has truly witnessed its beauty and touched upon its very essence. He has felt the mystery hidden amongst its ancient crevices and layered peaks. He has met some of the creatures who abide within and around its many unusual features and he has stood with me on the summit of Sheep Mountain Table and looked out across the lush green grasslands, leading to the Great Plains below. He has marvelled at the sun's dazzling early morning show and has watched the long shadows of an evening, amidst the radiance of a sunset's glorious glow. Two Feathers has felt his own soul blend into the wonder of this rugged land, which is a part of our home – and I as a father, have grown.

"Just Wild and Free"

With head held high and torso bare,
a single feather in long black hair,
the Indian sits astride his horse,
a mighty power . . . a gentle force.
He rides bare-back upon his steed,
moving at amazing speed,
his horse's hooves a muted sound
upon the grass along the ground.
With hair and mane blown in the breeze
he gallops full stretch, with simple ease.

He has the prairie for his home
and knows he never is alone,
for many creatures here abide
and buffalo roam far and wide.
The sun it leads him through the day,
the stars at night show him the way.
The rivers flow and quench his thirst
and on the bushes berries burst,
while rocks and soil beneath his feet
nourish him with food to eat.
He loves the forest with the trees
and hears each rustle in the leaves.
He knows the flowers by their name,
he smells the air and senses rain.
The mountains tall he views with awe,
they'll stand supreme, forever more.
The eagle soaring in the sky
will be his eyes from up on high.
The mountain lion is his guide
and tells him when to run, or hide.
He respects the land and all that's there,
each single breath he draws with care.
He sees all nature as a whole
. . . for in it is his very soul.
He knows the moon will greet the morn,
when he will worship quite alone
and of his own, within his mind,
he is at peace with all his kind.
His children know that he is there
to love, protect and treat them fair
and with his woman there's a bond
that is as tender, as is strong.

His Ancestors who've gone ahead
he knows live on - there are no dead,
for he is spirit on this Earth
learning lessons from his birth
and as the seasons come and go
his strength and knowledge gently grow.
Upon the plains he feels at one
with all that is and all that's gone,
his head held high for all to see
he's proud to be . . . just, wild and free.

3.9.94

"Just Children of Mother Earth"

I love Mother Earth . . . she is my Mother,
joining me with every other living thing that I may see,
no matter who, or what, they be. In her embrace I am a child,
a part of all I live beside and as a speck in her great flow,
she knows my needs and helps me grow. She lifts me
up when I am sad - encouraging me
when times are bad.

The four-leggeds I walk among, speak to
me in their own tongue. I sense their energies around,
above, upon and in the ground and when the song-bird sweetly
sings my spirit soars, I spread my wings to view the greatness
of the land - the woods and mountains, canyons grand,
hills and valleys, meadows green, the
open plains and prairie scene.

The untold beauty I embrace is Mother Earth's
natural face, but like an infant I must learn how fire
can warm - yet also burn. Respect is what lets me survive, for
all around me is alive . . . the rocks and stones, the air
I breathe, each grain of sand, all help to weave
the web of life in which I dwell. Through
love, I strive to serve them well.

The creatures with whom our lives unwind
are brothers of a different kind, their wisdom far outshines
my own, it is by watching them . . . I've grown. The rivers refresh
me, keep me calm, while trees give out a healing balm. The four
winds caress my soul within, like the moon and stars
when day grows dim, until the new dawn finally
breaks and once again - the World awakes.

The sun's great energy comforts all,
'tis Mothers Nature's healing shawl and she wraps
it round me, ever true, despite the traumas I go through,
for in my life I need to learn of good and bad, the truth to earn.
The sun's power touches everything, moving the seasons from
Spring to Spring and in its light is found re-birth,
sent by the Great Spirit - to Mother Earth.

Yes, Mother Earth is our mother . . .
and we are part of one another.

28.3.08

CHAPTER ELEVEN

The Ways of Our People

For generations our people have learned and remembered our way of life through the gentle art of storytelling, these precious accounts having been passed down from one person to the next. As well as being told by word of mouth, events are also shown in pictures painted on buffalo skins. These stories advise us on the right way to live – and they teach us well. Often they relate to the many animals with whom we share this wonderful land, for the Lakota believe all living things are connected and all are of Spirit. We know the creatures are wise for they have not forgotten the ways of the Great Spirit. We truly admire each one and we try to follow their different examples, whether they be the winged, the scaled, those of fur, feather or skin, whether they be the four or two-legged. We listen to our Mother the Earth and we draw closer to her through our simple understanding and respect of her natural forces. Each morning we honour the sun and in the evening we sit beneath the moon, our eyes drawn to the millions of stars above and to the far reaching Universe beyond. We listen intently to the four winds and to the pulse of the earth itself.

Although my own story is small, the story of my people is great. We the Lakota, or Sioux as the Whiteman often calls us, will come to be known as one of the most spiritual of all the Plains Indians. Our leaders are honest and just men. They treat everyone with dignity, whether they are of our own people who love and trust them, or the white people who continually lie to them. The names which I mention here are but a few – *Mahpiya Luta*, Red Cloud. *Tatanka Iyotaka*, Sitting Bull. *Tasunke Witko*, Crazy Horse and *Hehaka Sapa*, Black Elk. There are indeed many more great leaders, including those from the Cheyenne and other Tribes, but no matter our differences, we all live in complete harmony with Mother Nature.

I would like to tell you now about one of our most sacred rites. We have many ceremonies but the most important of them is *Wiwanyag Wachipi*, 'The Sun Dance' or to translate it more accurately – 'The Dance Looking at the Sun'. It was given to our people by White Buffalo Calf Woman, many years ago and has been passed down through the ages. Our Sun Dance is held in June every year, during the Moon of Fattening. The Sun Dance is performed as an offering of the Dancers' body and soul to *Wakan Tanka*, the Great Spirit. In this sacred ceremony the Dancers suffer, so they and their people may gain strength and further understanding. Those people who are not taking part send out prayers for the Dancers, as well as for their loved ones and themselves. They also sit quietly meditating. Sun Dances vary slightly, according to the personal thoughts of the Medicine Man whose Sun Dance it is.

There are many significant things in the Sun Dance, the foremost being the sacred Cottonwood Tree, *Waga Chan*. It is known as . . . the 'Rustling Tree' for its leaves will rustle in the slightest of breezes, as though it is whispering to you. One of the tallest trees around, out on the plains people use it as a marker, because of its tendency to grow near water. Another is our sacred drum which is made from buffalo hide. Its round form represents the Universe and its strong steady rhythm is the heart beating at the centre. Its sound is the voice of Wakan Tanka and this sound stirs the people, helping them to understand the mystery and power in all things. Buffalo skulls too, are used.

Tatanka the Buffalo is always treated with great respect, for the Lakota believe Tatanka is especially wise and can teach us so much. He is as a relative to us. Without him, the Indian would be no more. We also have our Sacred Pipes, Hoops and Staffs.

The Sun Dance Ceremony lasts for four days, but the many preparations for it start in mid-January. The day prior to it happening, is called the Tree Day. This is when the Dancers meet together and go with their Medicine Man out into the wilderness, to collect the Cottonwood Tree which he has previously chosen. Before this tree is taken from out of the earth, a special ceremony is performed in its honour. Once it has been cut, it is not acceptable for the tree to touch the ground until it is placed in the Sacred Circle. Therefore, we carry it high upon our shoulders to the site where our Sun Dance will be performed. On arriving there, an eight-foot-deep hole will have been dug and yet another ceremony marks the tree being put back into Mother Earth. It usually stands about thirty-two feet in height.

With the Sacred Cottonwood Tree safely positioned in the centre of the Circle, our different coloured ropes which we have tied to it, can be seen hanging down, close to its trunk. All the branches of the tree have been removed except for two large upper ones, which have two smaller off-shoots on each end. Prairie sage has been entwined around a large bough which has been secured across the space where the two main branches divide up and outwards. It is to this, the Dancers' ropes are firmly attached. Above is fastened yet another branch over which hangs a much thicker rope, one end of it being tied to a long sturdy bough that stands upright on the ground, resting against the tree's trunk. This ancient scene is truly resplendent, for the tree also has ribbons hanging down from the four smaller branches left at the very top. These ribbons are of blue, red, yellow and white and strips of cloth in the same colours are hung above them. Around the base of the tree are placed more coloured cloths and tobacco ties. We use tobacco as a medicine, for like prairie sage, it possesses healing properties.

Our Sacred Dance Circle measures seventy-five feet across. Around the edge, marking its boundary, are more tobacco ties carefully fastened onto long pieces of twine. At our last Sun Dance, Two Feathers who was then almost thirteen years old, made four hundred and one of these tobacco ties, skilfully tying them into the twine. If, while he was doing this, the twine had broken, he would have had to start making it again from the beginning. As with the tree ribbons and cloths hanging high above, they are in the four colours of the Lakota Nation . . . with white to the south side of our Circle, yellow to the east, red to the north and blue instead of black, to the west. During the Sun Dance and other Sacred Ceremonies, blue replaces the colour black. Relatives and close friends who are invited to come and support the Dancers, sit beneath a branched canopy. This is constructed around the outside of the north and south edge of the Sun Dance Circle and is approximately seven feet high and ten feet wide. Although it is acceptable for people to wander around during the Dancers' rest periods . . . it is made clear that nobody should cross the East Entrance. If this did happen, it could alter the flow of energies into the Sacred Circle.

On the evening of the Tree Day, food is shared with everyone and this is the last meal the Dancers have until the Sun Dance has ended. During their four days of dancing, they do not eat – nor do they drink. Neither do they have any further close contact with their family, for they will now live in the tipis which are in a compound to the west side of the Circle. In this same compound there are also two Sweat Lodges with two special tipis placed either side of them. On the north side stands the Pipe Tipi and to the south the Fire-Keepers'. The sacred fire, which is built infront of the Sweat Lodges, has to be kept alight at all times. If, for any reason the fire should go out . . . the Sun Dance is over. If the sun disappears and the rain comes . . . the Sun Dance ends. Traditions must be adhered to and those whom the Medicine Man has allowed to be present at this sacred ritual, need to be suitably dressed. Though the weather is exceedingly hot, out of respect our women will cover their shoulders with a long-sleeved top and most carry a shawl. No-one is permitted to drink or eat anything in sight of the Dancers. Nor should any spectator wear any kind of charm, because it could affect the energies. Everybody, including the children who are there, are fully aware that the ground in and around the Circle – is sacred.

Our male Dancers are bare-chested and clothe themselves in long skirts. These are left open down one side, in order to help them stay cool. Sage anklets and wrist bands are worn and a circle of prairie sage is placed upon each one's head. Some of the men have sprigs of sage sticking out above their forehead, shielding them a little from the sun. The prairie sage, as mentioned before, is used for its healing and calming properties. In their headband the men wear two large eagle feathers which stand upright, one on either front side. All eagle feathers are sacred to our people. In this instance these two feathers are symbolic of antenna, receiving strength from the sun and the surrounding energies. An eagle bone whistle attached to a thin cord, hangs around their neck and is there for them to blow whilst they are dancing. This helps with their concentration, which in turn, gives them extra strength. The women Dancers are also dressed in long skirts and wear long-sleeved tops. They too have sage around their heads and adorn themselves with sage wrist and anklet bands, but they do not wear any eagle feathers upon their heads. Both women and men carry their own Sacred Pipe. It is safely cradled in the nook of one arm held horizontally across, in front of their body, until it is placed on the Pipe Rack within the Circle. Any children who dance are male and are therefore dressed like the men, but they do not carry a pipe, nor do they have eagle feathers. Every Dancer, unless barefooted, wears leather or beaded moccasins.

As we see the sun rising, we hear the drum sending forth its powerful beat. All the Dancers file in through the East Entrance and dance around the inner edge of the Sacred Circle before moving into four lines, radiating outwards from the centre. Facing the Cottonwood Tree, each line moves towards it, allowing every Dancer in turn to touch the tree, before going to their next place in the Circle. The children stand in a short line, facing the East. Everyone dances all the time. It is a gentle step with the feet continually being lifted up and down. The Dancers' hands, held out before them, make little movements from the wrists, as if they are shaking an imaginary rattle. Even when not moving around, this dance is still performed on the spot. Some of the people who are watching will at times also dance, but unlike the Dancers, they are fortunate to be standing in the shade beneath the wooded bower. They take care to keep in time with the beating of the drum.

After ninety minutes, all the Dancers move to the south of the Circle where one of them hands sage across the tobacco ties, to a spectator. He in turn brings other spectators forward to stand in a line, outside the Circle but facing the Dancers. The handing over of the Pipes then takes place between certain Dancers and those in this line. Burning sage is constantly being wafted around and its aromatic smell is both refreshing and uplifting. Next, the Dancers move to the west of the Circle, where any remaining pipes are left stacked neatly against the pipe rack, near to where the Staffs and Sacred Hoops are standing. This signals the time for the Dancers to go out through the West Entrance, to rest in the tipis. It will now be around seven in the morning, the sun having risen at five o'clock. Those spectators who have been handed the Pipes, offer them around. They keep relighting them, holding the pipe bowl for people, as each one takes their turn to join in and smoke. Remember, the sacred tobacco acts as a healing balm...for even those who are watching can be affected by the intense heat.

After half an hour the Dancers slowly come back in through the West Entrance and start dancing again, around the inner perimeter of the Circle. A Buffalo Hide has now been spread out upon the ground at the west side of the Tree. On some Dancers, red circles have been drawn on their chest or back and some of the women have had holes cut into the top part of their sleeves. In turn, seven of the male Dancers who have these red marks, are summoned to the centre. After walking around the Tree, they reach out their hand to touch it, before turning to stand with their back against its trunk. As they look up at the sky, they draw in the energies. The Medicine Man's helpers surround this Dancer on either side, whilst the Medicine Man and an Elder stand upon the buffalo hide in front of him. They brush the red circles with sage and the Dancer's skin is pierced twice on each side of his chest. Then smooth wooden pegs which the Dancer has previously made, are pushed through each of these cuts. The lower end of the Dancer's rope is untied from the Tree and now attached to these pegs in his chest. This may seem brutal but I have to say... no, it is all done with such care and tenderness. My people have been performing the Sun Dance for many, many generations. It is a dance of selfless suffering for the love of one's people.

Gently, the Dancer is led backwards away from the centre, his rope trailing from him. Securely tied to the Tree, he resumes dancing. One of the seven is pierced twice through his back. While this is happening the others continue dancing to the encouraging beat of the drum. The singers are softly chanting, the Dancers are blowing on their eagle bone whistles and the women are making the tremolo. All this is to show their support. Everything is so harmonious and very reassuring and the love one can feel is incredible. Smudging often takes place, the burning sage being wafted around not only the Dancers, but also around the people who are watching. At certain times the Dancers will move across the Circle to the four different directions until eventually, they all file out of the West Entrance and into the Compound. Only the seven who are pierced stay resting by the Sacred Cottonwood Tree, still attached to their ropes.

When the Dancers next emerge, they dance slowly around the inside of the Circle before gradually quickening their pace. This time their Sun Dance Leader, the Medicine Man, walks to the Tree and is pierced through his back, this being done by one of the Elders. The Dancers now dance more intensely as their Medicine Man, who is facing outwards, keeps dancing backwards to the tree and then out again. Each time he moves away from the centre, his rope is pulled more and more taut behind him. Everyone is chanting and eventually he does a special dance before lunging forward. The atmosphere at this particular moment, is *so* vibrant. His family stand facing him on the outside of the Sacred Circle. Suddenly, with an extra surge of energy, he lunges forward yet again – and breaks free from his rope, which rebounds back to the other side of the Tree, the pegs having been ripped from his skin. After this, other Dancers are pierced and they do the same. The original seven who were first pierced, move in and out with them, but do not try to break free. After every session the burning of sage and the exchanging of Pipes takes place. Sometimes, later in the afternoon, a family may be taken to the Tree for special healing and to receive a blessing.

Just before the sun sets at around quarter past seven, the day's dancing draws to a close. However, the seven who had been the first ones pierced earlier that morning, still remain tied to the tree. For the last time that day the Pipe Ceremony is performed, this time by the women. In a little while all the Dancers come back into the Circle and line up facing the east. Then they file out of the East Entrance and quietly walk round the back of the branched canopy, to the tipis in the Compound. This is how the Sun Dance continues for the next two days, but on the last day . . . other things will also take place.

The children who dance are allowed to go to their families during each of the rest periods. They do not dance all day and none of them are pierced. During any Sun Dance Ceremony people will at times, need help. Sometimes, if a new Dancer is unable to break free from his rope, one of the children who is dancing will be asked to stand quietly in front of him. The mere presence of this little one then gives this Dancer the extra encouragement he needs. All of the Dancers are carefully prepared for this Sacred Rite and their participation is completely voluntary. I can clearly remember my first Sun Dance as a young man, so many years ago. On that occasion I was not pierced . . . for I was there to gain the experience of taking part. I felt truly honoured to be dancing for those of my kind. In the months before, I recall my father guiding me in the making of an eagle bone whistle. He also helped me to make my own Pipe. Its stem was carved from wood and the bowl from stone. The Sacred Pipe represents truth and is always smoked when Treaties are being made. Maybe this is the reason why the Whiteman calls it – the 'Peace Pipe'. No matter, for it truly is a pipe of peace.

On the fourth and final morning the women are pierced but unlike the men, they are not attached to the Tree. They are pierced on the top of one arm and have the quill end of small eagle feathers gently pushed through the two cuts. These feathers hang downwards and are removed early in the afternoon. Also on this morning, a Dancer will be pierced twice on each side of his back. He is then attached to the thicker rope which has been hanging over the very top of the Tree, its other end still tied to the branch standing upright against the trunk. Seven Dancers take hold of this heavy branch in their arms and walk slowly backwards with it. As three others carefully lift the one who has just been pierced, the seven continue walking backwards, pulling him up into the air. He now hangs from the Sacred Tree, suspended on his rope from the two pegs in his back. He stays like that for almost a minute, until he is lowered gently down into the arms of the three who had helped to raise him up. Slowly, they escort him back to his place in the circle of Dancers. Again the loving support from everyone around can be felt flowing through the air.

Next, two male Dancers who have been pierced on their upper backs, take it in turn to walk clockwise around the outside of the Circle. They have been connected from the pegs in their back to the twelve buffalo skulls which are lying tied together in a long line. They lean forward holding onto a Staff with one hand, a Staff which has large eagle feathers running all down one side. As this Dancer slowly drags the skulls around the outside of the Circle, two other Dancers walk either side of him quietly offering words of encouragement. Another five Dancers guide the skulls along the ground using a branch. To perform his task, the Dancer is walking completely bent forward . . . even a single buffalo skull is heavy. As he struggles to make his way around the outside perimeter, his fellow Dancers in the Circle turn outwards, to face him. They do this to show their respect for what he is managing to achieve and to mentally urge him onwards. He is permitted to rest briefly when he reaches each of the four directions – North, East, South and West. When he finishes this ordeal, his family gather round to congratulate and comfort him. They are permitted to do so because he is still on the outside of the Dance Circle. Carefully, he is unfastened from the ropes and somehow finds the strength to walk freely around the outer perimeter, before resuming his place amongst the other Dancers. The second man then moves forward to do the same thing. As the Ceremony continues, others will be suspended from the Sacred Tree and more will take it in turn to pull the buffalo skulls around the outside of the Circle.

During the late afternoon, everybody watching is invited to draw closer to the outer edge. This is to receive healing from all the Dancers, who will move slowly around the inner perimeter, softly touching each person's head with their hand or with a Sacred Fan made from four large eagle feathers. Others will use a short Staff, while some women Dancers use their small Sacred Hoop. Every Dancer will stand facing each person for about thirty seconds. As already mentioned, during the Sun Dance a few Dancers will need help themselves, perhaps having collapsed due to the intense heat. However, the Medicine Man, as well as performing all his other duties, will be there watching over them. He has to be strong mentally, physically and spiritually. There are many things the Dancers must try to remember. For example, whenever it is necessary for anyone to move across the Circle, they should always go around the Sacred Tree – and this has to be done in a clockwise direction. They should never cut across from one side to the other. Again, the Medicine Man will always notice if they need reminding of such things. His guidance is constantly there for them.

Many times they dance in and out, moving continually from the perimeter to the centre and back out again, before those still tied to the Tree start breaking loose. Eventually, when they are all free from their ropes, it is time for the Ending Ceremony and the Dancers go towards the Tree for the last time, where they form a line facing south. A number of the men kneel down in two parallel lines with two of the young boys at the front. Their

Medicine Man then walks slowly between these lines to exchange the Pipe for the last time. The Drum beats very gently with a slow steady sound and a tender song is sung. The Medicine Man thanks everybody for their support and healing thoughts. A young boy dressed just like the Dancers, stands under the bower by the Drum and softly sings a Lakota prayer. This is so emotional – and the emotion is carried over as the Prayer Ties are gathered in from around the perimeter of the Circle.

After this has been done an Elder steps forward and thanks the Medicine Man, before he returns to his Dancers, who are in the tipis. Suddenly, the voice of the Medicine Man is heard calling out from the Tipi Compound, as he leads all his Dancers back into the Circle – "Come on everyone . . . you are going home." As the Dancers move into four lines and stand facing the east, little children with their mothers are invited into the Circle and line up opposite them. Then older children and other people join in. Some of the Dancers perform individual dances in the space between themselves and these loved ones. This time they leap and twirl, moving all around. Next the children dance, until everyone stands to one side as the Dancers file out of the East Entrance and around the outside of the wooded bower.

After four long days, the Sacred Sun Dance has now ended. It is time for everyone to be reunited with their families. There is a joyous feeling of celebration, although at first, some Dancers explain how they still feel – "Very much a part of somewhere else." They are not fully back. Everyone hugs each other. Later, all share in a special meal with their loved ones and although the Sun Dance for that year is over, it is an experience the Dancers will never forget. It is something quite primitive in its way . . . but also something which is very emotional and very spiritual. I know after any Sun Dance, for the next several days I wake up every morning with the sound of the eagle bone whistles in my head and the beat of the Drum in my heart. I can recall them still . . . and I always will.

>>>> <<<<

"Just Memories of the Sun Dance"

The Sun Dance, powerful and strong
with rhythmic beat of drum and song.
The Cottonwood Tree, standing tall,
reaching out to one and all.
The Dancers, proud to be a part
of what lies deep inside their heart.
The Medicine Man, good and true,
guiding all in what they do.
The Elders, standing quietly near,
fully focused . . . and sincere.
The Eagle Bone whistles, sharp and shrill,
helping each their quest fulfil.
The Sacred Pipe, Staff and Hoop,
the 'Tremolo' or sudden 'Whoop'.
The Buffalo Skulls upon the ground,
the smell of sage, wafted around.
The loving thoughts of each one there,
gently mingling into prayer.
The coloured cloths and tobacco ties,
an Eagle, who above us flies.

The Sacred Fire kept alight
throughout the day . . . and the night.
The Sweat Lodge, offering relief,
with its healing bringing sleep.
The Tipis, for those who wish to be
encircled in their harmony.
The comfort drawn from Mother Earth,
there for all - whate'er their worth.
The Sun Dance, powerful and strong,
renewing our Ancestral bond.

15.7.05

"Just the Words of the Whispering Cottonwood Tree"

Just a Cottonwood Tree standing tall
with rustling leaves that talk to all –
who'll pause to listen and heed my call.

For I whisper secrets from long ago
whenever the gentlest breezes blow,
telling what others need to know.

I recall the scenes that I once saw
of people caught in a mindless war,
waged against Nature and Natural Law.

The slaughter of creatures from all around,
the laying of tracks across open ground,
the plundering of land so wealth could be found.

A clashing of ways - of right and wrong,
people forced to move from where they belong
because of their colour and different tongue.

The breaking of Treaties . . . whatever they be,
ignoring even, the smallest plea,
imprisoning a Nation, who lived so free.

Yet - I have the sun and the life-giving rain,
the company of creatures who live yet again
and the love of a people who suffered such pain.

One day, perhaps, I'll no longer abide
out on the prairie or wooded hillside,
but stand in a Sun Dance, my heart filled with pride.

Decorated with ribbons and clothed in sweet sage,
I will witness a scene, passed down through an age . . .
and support all the Dancers who take centre stage.

I will carry their ropes and send out to each mind,
my own special strength as they seek now to find
the courage to dance for those of their kind.

The Sun Dance is sacred and those who take part
must nurture the love that exists in their heart,
love that can heal - and grant a fresh start.

As my life nears its end, my spirit moves free
to help those who once listened or danced around me
. . . a Sacred, yet humble, Cottonwood Tree.

16.2.06

"Just Words from the Elders"

Although it is so long ago we
walked this Earthly Sphere,
we still strive hard to join with you
and talk with those now here.
Across the ether and through time
our spirit reaches out
to try and bring new hope to all,
to chase away the doubt
- the doubt that life continues
and holds within its flow
the many thoughts and blessings,
which loved ones can bestow.

We offer you our wisdom,
to dry your many tears,
knowing happiness is there
for those with open ears.
Accept the age old teachings,
follow Natural Law,
blend within true learning
from those who've gone before . . .
those loved ones from the Spirit Realms
- ancestors, friends and guides,
the ones who understand you,
who listen to your cries.

Our rights were once denied us,
the land taken away,
our customs were rejected
. . . injustice ruled the day,
our young became disheartened,
their freedom was curtailed,
other's words were but a lie -
their promises all failed.
We knew of such great hardship,
we suffered for so long
and yet within that suffering,
our spirit grew more strong.

Remember, all are brothers
beneath Earth's spacious skies,
for deep inside each one of us
the spirit spark abides,
that Spark is the Great Spirit
- the Father of us all
and so it is we all are bound
within his Spirit Law.
Go out now, look around you,
search for the ones to help
you rise above the heartache
. . . towards a better self.

10.2.03

143

CHAPTER TWELVE

Bear Lodge, Mato Tipila

Our only son, Two Feathers, is in a group of seven who are riding to Bear Lodge, a natural structure which rises up out of the Great Plains of Wyoming. Running Water, just like the other mothers, is quite anxious but knows it is a part of his development and will help him progress from an inexperienced youth, to a fully independent young man. This group are all in their fourteenth summer and are accompanied by two of our Tribal Elders, who will offer them guidance and protection while they spend time outside our village, travelling through a beautiful but demanding and unpredictable wilderness. Mato Tipila is to the northwest of the Black Hills and is sacred to us and others of our kind. It has a very special place in our hearts. It is where we can seek spiritual upliftment and receive teachings from those no longer here, but who still relate to us from their spirit homes. It has been important to our people for many years, years which go far back, to a time when our lands stretched from ocean to ocean and all the different Tribes lived contented and free.

I have been told in a vision that one day the Whiteman will rename this sacred place and refer to it as 'Devils Tower', but that is not what we call it – and not what it was called in the past. This is an ignorant name, given by ignorant men. Mato Tipila or Bear Lodge, is a place of wonder and legend. It is where seven sisters were saved from a Great Bear. They were being chased by him, but before coming to any harm they managed to reach the stump of a huge tree. The tree called to them to climb upon it and as they did so it rose upwards with a great force, up towards the sky. It raised them clear of the bear's massive claws. There they felt safe, but the bear reared up against the tree and his claws scored the bark all around. The sisters were then lifted to the heavens above, where each became a star. It is to this sacred spot that our young men now go, carrying with them our love and encouragement.

Our sons are travelling out there to hold their first Vision Quest and after arriving in its foothills, they will go their own separate ways. The following four days and nights will be spent in meditation and prayer, relating not only to the Great Spirit but to other spirits... perhaps even that of the Great Bear. This is to give each one the opportunity to learn of their own special Spirit Animal and to form a bond between them which once made, will last forever. They have now safely journeyed across the green prairie, moving slowly up through Wyoming and the Powder River country. Everyone is feeling good, their bodies strong and healthy. As their horses move swiftly over the soft earth, each rider is aware of the wind in his hair and the sun shining down. They call out in song, for what great joy it is to feel so free. In the distance the outline of Mato Tipila can suddenly be seen, its well-known shape standing tall and proud. The day is fine and the weather clear. Together, they heartily send forth another cheer.

Before moving up into the foothills surrounding Bear Lodge, a meal will be shared and so they dismount. A white-tailed deer is grazing not too far away and thanks are offered to Wakan Tanka for this precious gift of food. Kneeling in the undergrowth, they quietly study their prey... then send out prayers as their arrows take aim, asking that its spirit be quickly released from its physical frame. The thought of full bellies heightens their mood, for during their Vision Quest they will neither drink nor eat, allowing their bodies to slow down and their unconscious mind to rise to the fore. They wonder about the days to come, hoping their Special Spirit will connect and take them travelling across a far different plain, allowing brief glimpses of what their lives may hold. They think upon what important experiences might be gained and what these new adventures may unfold. Each understands how our body is only a shell, our Spirit being the true source of life. Nothing is known for certain, but we are taught that the course we take here on the Earthplane, will determine our worth when we move back into the Spirit World. There, the light of our inner-self will be unfurled.

The moon has risen and the stars shine brightly. Thoughts drift back to the previous night when at home in Long Grass Creek, together they built a sweat lodge in which to prepare themselves for the trials lying ahead. Our sweat lodges, as with our tipis, are rounded like the nest of a bird. Their true name is 'Purification Lodge' and it is in them we hold our Inipi Ceremony, a ritual which enables us to purify both body and mind. When large heated stones from the fire outside were carried in and cold water from the nearby creek poured over them, our sons had sat naked in the steam. Prayers were then said. Everyone needed to think on what their own Vision Quest may mean. Now our sons are sitting out in the foothills of Bear Lodge. The night air is refreshingly cool and all sleep well. Two Feathers dreams of the things which he hopes to be able to tell, when the four days are over and he will ride home. Will he and his friends be the same – or will they return as grown men?

Just before daybreak everyone is awake and the two Elders take charge of the ponies. Together, all share in a hearty breakfast and afterwards blessings are given to each one as they enjoy their last drink of water before starting out on their own. For a Vision Quest, we must be alone. Wishing the others well, one by one they leave the security of their camp. In this new found freedom, Two Feathers feels truly exhilarated. They have been instructed to make their way to Mato Tipila and once there, to touch its fluted rock sides, the lines of which run vertically upwards to its flat top. My son moves swiftly through the trees where he is sheltered from the heat of the sun, having left the openness of the prairie behind. His body is relaxed and to his fate, he is resigned. There is danger here, for the cougar, although elusive, is known to be around. It is him we fear most. At times our son can be rather impulsive, but he does value his life and so as well as carrying his flute, he also carries a knife. It is mid-summer and the young men are bare-chested, wearing only a breech cloth made from soft leather. On their feet are moccasins, my son's being a gift from his mother. Around his upper arms are amulets, both decorated with porcupine quills . . . this is one of his uncle's finest skills. Hanging from his neck on a piece of neatly woven twine, is a bear's tooth which I found long ago. It was lying in an old riverbed, almost hidden by pebbles. I hoped it might please the Great Bear for my son to honour him thus.

Having at last reached the boulders near to the base of Bear Lodge, Two Feathers moves skilfully through them and over the rough broken stone. Hidden in the numerous crevices and holes beneath his feet live black widow spiders and various kinds of snakes. Our children are taught never to forget how Mother Earth is the home of all who may roam here. The two-legged would do well to remember this. If we show respect to each creature, we will have less to fear. Two Feathers now finds himself standing next to Bear Lodge, this huge mound rising out of the earth. He feels so small compared to its massive size – just like a tiny ant moving around a large rock lying upon the ground. His attention is immediately drawn to the beautiful colours of Mato Tipila which are orange, brown, yellow and grey. Even though the rock is old, its colours have not faded and they certainly resemble the shades taken from the trunk of a tree. The deeply scoured lines running down the sides are indeed vertical and straight.

After staring intently into this multi-coloured wall of rock, Two Feathers looks slowly up. Higher and higher his eyes now gaze until he can see the edge of its summit towering high above him, almost lost in the haze. He watches as four large birds circle silently around, their silhouettes standing out clear against the blue sky. Their effortless flight makes him inwardly sigh. Looking down again at the colours in front of him, his hand reaches out to caress the rock and its rough ridges. Doing this brings a sensation of pure energy surging through his body, touching his soul as it races along. He is held in its greatness and in its sheer power. For a while he stands quite still, totally transfixed, before chanting his appreciation to Father Sky and Mother Earth – they who are the givers of life and who sanctioned his birth.

Although the light has started to fade, the sun is still shining and yet again our son is mesmerised by all the beauty surrounding him. Turning to watch the fallen leaves dancing through the glade he truly feels a part of this incredible place, as if long-lost memories are lingering there for him to recall. The air has become much cooler and Two Feathers is aware of a cold breeze blowing against his legs. Suddenly, he realises that what has seemed like only minutes, has in fact been many hours. Whilst there, in that sacred place … time ceased to exist. As the darkness of night slowly falls, with an added caution in his step, he descends through the trees on the sloping hillside. Nearing the edge of the woodland he finds a hollow in which to settle and sleep – and without any undue hesitation, closes his eyes.

A fresh new dawn comes and goes and yet he slumbers on, until his senses are awakened by a shuffling in the bushes close by. Slowly he partially opens his eyes. All his instincts are telling him to keep very still . . . and to survive, it is often wise to follow their will. I believe instincts come from what our spirit is trying to tell us and I have often found out – it is best to obey. Everyone has free will but, it is usually good to heed that small inner voice. However, this time there is no real cause for alarm. The noise he heard in the bushes is only a red fox looking for an easy meal. Two Feathers continues to conceal his own presence by staying motionless, for something deep inside is saying . . . there are other eyes watching him. He notices a large cottontail rabbit crouching down low. He hopes the rabbit will come to no harm for it is trying so hard to avoid being caught. Thankfully, the young fox is not that keen. He is far too impatient and wanders off. The cottontail lives to see the next day. Two Feathers feels the quickened rhythm of his own heartbeat. This small incident has revealed to him just how vulnerable we all are. Before getting to his feet, he pauses to scan the woodland around. It is so important to stay alert, for the last thing he needs is to be hurt. Due to how long he slept, the early hours of the morning have gone. Two Feathers is eager to pursue his journey.

The air is again turning hot as he makes his way out of the trees, moving towards some small buttes where it is easier to travel. Walking along the banks of a stream, he smiles to himself as he watches two river otters playfully chasing each other. It is good to share in their joy and he makes himself comfortable by relaxing against the trunk of a Silver Birch tree, for it is an ideal place to stop. Listening to the many birds chirping above him in its branches, he feels contented and safe. However, as an added precaution he presses down the long grass around where he will sit. This should deter any snakes from coming too near, as they feel very exposed and vulnerable in short scrub. Closing his eyes, he humbly asks for added protection before withdrawing into a deeper state of mind. Over the longer grasses flies a meadow lark and her uplifting song adds to the serenity which is starting to unfold. He is sure there is nothing to fear, for an elk herd is quietly grazing further downstream and he knows if any predators were to appear, the older elk would certainly start to panic and bark.

After a few hours of meditation and playing on his flute, Two Feathers decides to find somewhere more protected to spend the night. It is late afternoon and the blueness of the sky is changing to a dark grey. There is definitely a smell of rain blowing his way and out on the open prairie, both man and creature are much more vulnerable to the elements. Only a few hours of daylight are now left in which to find a sheltered place. Before leaving, he raises up his arms and turning to face the tree against which he sat, thanks it most sincerely for the healing he has received. He also sends forth kind words for his brothers and sisters – the otters, birds and elk, wishing them safety through the long hours of the oncoming night. They have quietly retreated out of sight into a small secluded dell. He thinks of his human family back here in our village and asks Wakan Tanka to keep everyone safe.

Next day, our son is walking happily through an outcrop of boulders and rock when, for no apparent reason, tiny cold shudders start to run down his spine. His inner-self immediately warns him to stop . . . and he does so, just in time, for something ahead is giving him cause for concern. Close to the ferns in front of his feet is a clear paw mark, one which he has learned to respect, a track which undoubtedly tells him it is from a big cat. This imprint is rounded and the width of his hand. There are no claw marks to be seen but showing clearly is the outline of four toes and a large pad. It is quite intimidating, for this paw mark speaks of stealth and might. Trying to look down the narrow pathway ahead, he regrets the fact that dusk has fallen and the light is bad. Then just a little further along the track, his eyes pick out a female cougar standing slightly off to the right. He freezes – but not in his mind, for all his senses are fully alert. His hand slowly reaches for his knife, though a full encounter he is hoping to avoid. The cougar stretches her neck and raises her head, sniffing the slight breeze which is blowing her way. The air bearing his scent is drawn in through flared nostrils, opened so wide. Every part of his being comes alive as he prays that she has no cubs with her. Though wanting to keep fully focused on the cougar, our son's eyes are darting here and there. He begins to feel a little more at ease, for he can detect no other movement around, but he needs to be sure. If she does have cubs, hopefully they have gone to ground, for if any were to appear – it is quite likely a fight would ensue.

This large powerful cat stands perfectly still, blending into the woodland's shade. Although afraid, Two Feathers finds it impossible not to admire her beauty and the unquestionable courage shown in her watchful eyes. What wisdom lies therein. What awe her presence inspires. He continues looking straight at her and breathes in deeply. He must not run, stoop low or turn his back, for any of these movements would trigger her instincts to attack. Our children, even when still young, are taught that if they encounter a mountain lion or lynx, they should attempt to make themselves look larger . . . and therefore more fearsome. This, however, must always be done with great care and only with the slowest of movements. Without changing his gaze, Two Feathers stretches out one arm to break off some slender branches from a shrub, growing nearby. Lifting these up above his head, such tactics he nervously tries. Thankfully, our son keeps reminding himself not to panic, or run. It is necessary for him to stay strong for clear thinking to flow and even though deep inside he is shaking, he knows he must not show any fear, because this she would sense and his weakness then know. He talks very softly, telling her they are friends . . . friends who share this wild domain and that it is not in his mind to hurt her, nor any of her kind. Nor does he wish to invade her space.

He takes another deep breath, for now is the time to compose himself and move steadily away. With the utmost caution, he retreats slowly backwards whilst asking the Great Spirit to shield them both from any distress. Like the brave cottontail rabbit seen the previous day, he tries very hard to stay calm. Although his retreat is slow it is obvious any movement is not to the cougar's liking, for she starts to crouch down low. This is not a good sign. He stops and stands still. In his thoughts he begins to ponder on how long they will both stay there, looking so intently at each other . . . and he cannot help thinking of his sister and parents. To not run, takes all of his will. Then without any warning she turns away and making no fuss, nor even the slightest noise, walks gracefully down the wooded path ahead, until she disappears from sight. He is so impressed with her elegance, beauty and poise and so grateful it has not been necessary to face a mother cougar's protective wrath.

Reasoning tells him to wait for as long as possible before continuing along this meandering track, allowing her time to move further on. The daylight though, has almost gone and he dare not hesitate any longer. His desire to find safety is now so strong. The rest of that evening proves to be quite uneventful, enabling Two Feathers to get far enough away to feel it is safe to settle down and sleep. Before doing so, he sends out thoughts for his feline friend and again thanks Wakan Tanka for his unseen help. Vital lessons are continually being learnt. This one inspired not only quick thinking but courage and lots of patience. It also made him realise how, when in danger, we need to slow our breathing down in order to stay in complete control, for any impulsiveness only causes other problems to unfold. As the bright sun awakens him the next morning, his dreams of the mountain lion have not gone away. In his heart he respects and admires her still, but it will take a while longer before the memory of his fear completely goes, for it was very intense to stare so deeply into her piercing eyes. To avoid a similar experience, he decides it is best to settle himself down near to this place where he stayed safe throughout the previous night. Soon his time around Mato Tipila will sadly come to an end.

Climbing the south face of a not too challenging butte, Two Feathers stares confidently out across the vast sunlit plains, towards Bear Lodge. Today will be spent in further meditation, trying to fulfil his Vision Quest by hopefully getting in touch with his own special spirit friend. However, his whole body is aching for something to eat and he tries hard to fight against this, by playing his flute. Perhaps its sound may block out his awful yearning for food. The flow of the music does seem to help, taking his mind back to the comfort of our family tipi and his mother's tender caress. Then, drawing on added strength by sending out thoughts to me, his father, the sharper hunger pains start to soften and slowly become less. It is not in our people's nature to accept defeat but at that particular moment . . . even a few small berries would have seemed like a treat. The notes from his sacred flute are greatly uplifting, for they have the power to ease torment of any kind. Two Feathers and his friends have been instructed that if they feel really ill, they must take a few sips from a clear running stream or drink rain water found trapped in nearby rocks. Although he desperately hopes to avoid doing this – only time will tell. Our sons know above all, they must stay fit and in control.

The playing of his sacred flute is indeed calming and its slow lilting sound sends him into a meditative state, enabling his spirit loved ones to draw closer and soothe him even more. They take him away . . . to where he's not sure, but he can feel the rush of cool air and hear the faint beat of a drum. Their love is beyond compare. They quietly lift him up higher and higher until over the trees he flies, above the buttes and lush woodlands, out across the prairie towards a place quite safe and serene. Suddenly, as though from a great height, he is looking down on what appears to be an island raised up from the wide valley floor – and recognises it as the top of Bear Lodge, over which he is now soaring. Although his travelling has been at such a rapid pace, all at once it lessens and he gently descends. Perhaps here on this high plateau, his quest will succeed. Standing on the summit he calls out for his spirit friend. His voice echoes loud and clear, as if it were bouncing from cloud to cloud. How long he stayed he cannot say, but when he came back into his body . . . the day was drawing to a close. Evening had begun and his travelling had ended. Sleep came quickly that night, for all his tension and worries had found release.

As his fourth and final day started to dawn, Two Feathers opened his eyes and stretched and yawned. It was good to lie in the warmth of the sun, gazing up at the clouds and never-ending sky. However, the whole of him is feeling weak yet again, but he knows he must stay strong. There is still a vision to seek. That morning he is forced to accept that in order to regain his strength, he has no option but to stop and drink, thereby quenching his thirst. Common sense must overcome any foolish pride. It would do no good if he collapsed and possibly died, for that would achieve nought. These are the ideals he must follow. This is what is taught – and so struggling across a meadow towards a sparkling stream, he scoops up its fresh water and drinks slowly from his cupped hands, though only that small quantity his weakened body so desperately needs. Afterwards, while walking through the meadowland he sees patches of flattened grasses amongst the flowers and prairie sage. He realises these are where black bears have stopped for a while, to rest and feed their young. His steps are quickly retraced. He must settle himself in a more secluded place, to safely resume his Vision Quest.

We can but do our best – and turning to each of the four directions, Two Feathers asks the different winds to blow further awareness towards him, to help him discover with whom he will bond. He needs to meet this special spirit who will become his true friend. He plays his flute again to help guide them across from sphere to sphere. Hopefully this time they will recognise him and respond to his willingness for them to draw near. Fresh breezes begin to blow. They come from the south, yet they feel quite raw and he remembers that it was to there he travelled in meditation the day before, when he was taken to the summit of Bear Lodge. A large bird of prey flies across, just above him. Could this be his spirit friend? Nothing happens, so he raises up his arms and urges her to stop, but the bird flies further on and he knows – it is not.

Two Feathers sends out a final request to his spirit helpers, eagerly asking them once again to help him in his Vision Quest. The breeze starts to fade and a strange mist quietly descends ... he is certain this will bring his special spirit animal and strains to see more. Inside the misty white haze which is growing like a swirling storm, a definite shape is beginning to appear. It seems to be fairly large with a short pointed nose and upright ears. The eyes, though wary, are twinkling and a friendly expression starts to show through. The rest of its body is still trying to build up. Our son is so delighted for this image carries with it a great awareness. His mind is convinced this is going to be the creature who will be his spirit friend. Then, as the soft mist gradually clears, it is there, standing boldly in his view ... a young and handsome coyote pup. Two Feathers' breath is almost taken away and he stands transfixed, until a sudden fear overtakes him – that this image may not stay. He calls out in welcome, inviting it to draw closer and without any hesitation the coyote pup is there beside him. How wise are the ways of the Spirit World, their wisdom can never be denied. I know our son's curiosity can often lead him into trouble, yet Coyote is the Trickster . . . and can outwit any other. We know from the teachings of our people that this is so. Now, throughout the rest of his earthly journey, Two Feathers will have this spirit animal to share his life and when the time comes for him to return home to that land where life is eternal – they will travel there together, as faithful friends. That night our son is no longer alone. Coyote is with him and Two Feathers can even feel his body heat, for although he is of the spirit, he is so real when they meet. The pangs of hunger have subsided and on awakening, he is glowing with pure happiness.

Our son has been so fortunate, for even his encounter with the mountain lion went well. He truly had a lucky escape. What fantastic experiences have been given to him and what a wonderful freedom he has known. Nothing from these past few days will ever be wasted. All that has been felt, done or seen, will stay with him forever. Although there were certain times when I think maybe he could have conducted himself in a better way, or even been a little wiser in some of the more simpler decisions he made, it is with complete honesty that I feel he can say – he did try his very best. Meeting his spirit animal friend is excellent proof of the success of his first Vision Quest.

Two Feathers' spiritual journey touched him to the core for he had never previously known anything like it. He was positive that on his return the Elders of the village would invite him to take his place in our society, now he had proved himself. He also hoped his own family would be pleased with him. I know . . . I am. He must appreciate though – it will take more than a day to assess how well he has done. The words he received while sitting in meditation will be shared with the Elders and over the next few weeks he will be advised on how to correctly interpret their hidden meanings. Then they will help him plan how to improve not only his personal self, but his whole outlook towards others and to daily life. This in turn will encourage him to chase away undue fears, removing unnecessary stress. Both his mother and I sincerely hope those others who travelled with him, also achieved their desires and met with their special spirit animal. Our prayers are that they too have returned safely and that they will have all received upliftment and found a deeper insight and understanding of life.

The most important thing for Two Feathers is being aware that from this moment onwards, his spirit coyote is constantly there. He knows it is such a privilege to have this wonderful creature blend with him, for wherever he goes, Coyote will be his guide. Our son is now fully conscious of this loyal companion and of the added protection which he receives. Their bonding and continuing journey together will truly be a success. Although our special animal friends come from the Spirit Land and we are from this World, all are of Spirit . . . and when such mutual love is unfurled, it forms an unseen bridge which spans any differences. Make no mistake, the bond that is made, no-one can break. Whatever ills befall us will be lessened by their presence, for they will mentally lift us up from any sadness and be there for our defence against anything bad. We will share in their courage and learn from the wisdom they show. In total harmony both will move forward together as understanding grows. The love shown, one for the other, shall never end for our Spirit Animals are indeed, very special friends. Surviving his exciting and unique experience, which lasted for four days and four nights, has been quite a feat. We are forever grateful that the Great Spirit not only walked with our son, but sent him such a precious gift. Two Feathers' true oneness with Nature *and* with Bear Lodge . . . Mato Tipila, is now complete.

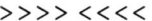

"Just Flying Free"

Take me through the canyons where time itself stands still,
to fly upon an Eagle's wing
that I may drink my fill,
let me touch the rock face and feel the power therein,
help me lift my senses, my
my journey to begin.

Take me into the woodlands to soar around each tree,
carried on the whistling wind
so happy to be free,
there I can greet the creatures who make the woods their home,
to join with them in harmony
and never feel alone.

Take me across the prairie, the grasslands stretching far,
to view the winding rivers
reflecting every star,
to watch the mighty buffalo, their awesome strength admire
and blend with Mother Nature . . .
what more could I desire.

Take me above the mountains where I may know the peace,
gliding with the buzzards -
my soul can find release,
rising ever higher, the air so sharp and clear,
then dropping to the valleys to
race with hare and deer.

Take me beyond the thoughts of now to where my Being sings,
to see and smell and touch and hear
and sense so many things,
to meet with those whom I have known, whose caring draws
me nigh, those friends who walked beside me,
in days that have gone by.

Take me within the quiet to let these moments grow,
to reach into the wilderness
and feel the healing flow,
behold their smiling faces, their words upon the air,
as we sit around the campfire
- sweet memories to share.

Take me across that open space to where my thoughts aspire
to rise above the earth and wind,
the water and the fire,
to taste the joy of being free . . . free to fly at will,
where dreams become reality and
time once more stands still.

7.2.00

"Just Welcoming a New Day"

When we first awake we should welcome the day
and ask for upliftment to brighten our way,
sending out thoughts for those whom we love . . .
those on the Earthplane and in realms above,
to help keep them safe, happy and free,
surrounded in light and true harmony.

We know spirit healing can reach far and near
upon waves of caring we send out sincere,
for those who are suffering . . . man, woman or child,
our animal friends and those of the wild.
We also send thoughts that this world will soon find
Nature's own cures for both body and mind.

We thank all our helpers and friends from afar
who guide us and guard us wherever we are,
releasing such feelings of genuine love
reminding us gently of how those above . . .
offer their guidance so we may stay strong
to follow what's right and dismiss what is wrong.

We pray that all peoples, no matter their creed,
can join in the truth and let friendship succeed,
that each can unite and eventually learn
to love all living things and find love in return.
May we open more eyes and more hearts in this way . . .
as we send out our thoughts and welcome the day.

28.2.02

"Just Refreshing Pauses"

Stop and pause . . . relax, unwind,
let Nature's beauty soothe your mind.

Stop and pause . . . whene'er you may,
allow your cares to melt away.

Stop and pause . . . look around,
see the dew upon the ground.

Stop and pause . . . just take the time
to smell the grass and woodland pine.

Stop and pause . . . and listen well,
hear the birdsong in the dell.

Stop and pause . . . to watch the stream
trickling through the meadow green.

Stop and pause . . . if you can,
perhaps to help your fellowman.

Stop and pause . . . sit down and view
those who are a part of you.

Stop and pause . . . then feel the sun
when your daily chores are done.

Stop and pause . . . banish all strife,
enjoy the simple things in life.

19.5.03

CHAPTER THIRTEEN

The Passing of Time

Life in our village carries on. Thankfully, our children are kept well nourished and enjoy the security of their homes. Our ponies remain healthy and present us with strong foals. The river as always flows ever onwards, its waters fresh and sparkling 'neath the rays of the sun. The forest continues to offer its protection to the many kinds of creatures who seek shelter therein. We still hear the beautiful, haunting cry of the wolves out on the prairie and just like in the past, at times they venture nearer, to refresh themselves in the cool pools found along the riverbank. My Hawk remains with me. He is a little slower now, for like myself, he too has grown old. He stays much longer by our tipi and is quite content to be fed more and more by me – but he still loves to soar into the blue of the sky and feel the wind against his face and the sunshine on his back. He never falters in his daring low swoops across the stream for his eyes remain bright and are as keen as ever. He misses nought, not the fall of a leaf nor the insect on the wing. I know he has fathered numerous offspring and on these occasions, he would spend time away with his mate. What a great friendship we have known, he and I. When we are together he continues to make me feel I too can fly . . . even if only in my dreams. I simply need to sit quietly with an open mind, to be able to visit wherever I please. In one's own eye, what wonders can be seen and in one's own thoughts, what one can achieve! It matters not the age we may be, nor how strong or active our body has stayed, for when in a meditative state we are free – and our spirit becomes both uplifted and refreshed.

Running Water and I are as much in love now as we have always been and still enjoy sitting close to each other by the waterfall, where we first met. Our children have grown into fine young adults and we have been blessed with three grandchildren. Two Feathers is a handsome and sensitive young man and we are so proud of him and his gentle wife. Their children provide plenty of laughter and fun, keeping us both feeling young. Our lovely daughter Dancing Stream, is as fair and innocent of mind as when she was born. Everybody is drawn to her and the caring nature she shows is one that reminds me of my mother. With encouragement and hard work, I have reached the position of Medicine Man and I am pleased how my own son is showing the qualities which will help him one day, to do the same. Although my parents are now with our Ancestors, we still converse with one another and the inspiration I receive from my grandfather is quite remarkable. I know without any doubt, they all live on and are reunited with my twin brother, Two Shadows. It makes me truly happy for them. I am also aware White Star often visits, for he and Two Shadows know each other well in that other world, just beyond our view.

Blazing Bow has become my close friend and never seems troubled or at all handicapped by having the use of only one arm. His positive attitude has certainly helped him to adapt and he sets a good example to all. We are fortunate that not only our own family, but our whole village and its people, still survive . . . for the Whiteman continues to plunder the land. No longer can our Tribes go out on the long treks we once used to enjoy. We can no longer wander freely across this beautiful and rugged land which we have always loved. We cannot go out onto the vast prairie and roam over the Great Plains, nor can we ride peacefully and without concern through the ever swaying grasslands, that are part of our natural abode. At times we do manage to travel north to the Black Hills and though reaching them is hazardous, they are one of the few places left where we can feel safe and free. The leaders of the Whites have finally accepted the sacredness of these tall mountains we honour and love and have banned their people from being there. We thank the Great Spirit for this being so.

The seasons of the sun and the wind, the rain and the snow, seem to come more quickly and yet, quite slowly go. We are in the late autumn of our years when my lovely Running Water passes on, but we are of the same … and I know for certain, she is not gone. She became extremely tired in the weeks leading up to her journey home. Though her lustre still shone – it was starting to fade. It was on a clear and crisp morning as the birds cheerfully sang, that I realised her spirit was ready and eager to move back into the sphere from whence it had come. She looked relaxed and peaceful, her face outlined in a beautiful glow. There was an extra radiance around her and I knew the Great Spirit was calling her home. Sitting beside her, like I had done so many times before, we smiled as I held her frail hand. I noticed my Hawk was quietly there. While the morning dew glistened in the soft rays of the sun, so I watched as her life on this Earthplane gently drew to its close. Of course I was sad, desperately sad … but the sadness I bore was for my own loss. I could not feel unhappy for her. I would never deny her the joyfulness she was now going to experience as she rejoined her many loved ones, already in that other sphere. Her physical body had grown old and weak but now she would once again become the lovely young girl I had met by the falls. I needed to keep my inner light bright and not hold her back, nor dampen her joy. Yet more tears filled my eyes and my emotions over-spilled as I suddenly realised … it was my Hawk who was guiding her home. He too had drawn his last breath in this place we call Earth. Together, their spirits had flown.

I knew I was privileged to witness what I did, for I could feel the presence of a great love flowing all around. I could see the most beautiful colours mingling in the air and from far, far away, I could hear the sound of a drum and the fluttering of wings. "Travel safely," I whispered. "Travel safely to that Light which is home, to that land where the mighty buffalo continue to roam free and where the streams constantly run and no malice is known." After a while, I know not how long, I sensed I sat there alone. Both had crossed that Great Divide. It was time for me to move and face the rest of the day . . . and indeed, the rest of my life without the earthly presence of the woman I always would love. Walking into the woodland and then deeper into the forest, I lost myself in the healing given from the trees. It touched my Soul and calmed me within, lessening my pain – the pain we all feel when a loved one steps over to continue their life in that other world. It hurts, no matter what we know and believe. I had to think on the fact there was still the physical presence of my daughter and son and of my grandchildren, whom I loved dearly and who meant so much to me. There would always be the images of Running Water forever in my heart and I only needed to look up with eyes closed, to hear the beating of the feathered wings of my good friend, the Hawk. I knew without any doubt, they would always be there for me and that one day, when the Great Spirit called my name, they would both welcome my spirit home. The greatest wish I have now is that when my time comes, my loved ones here on the Earthplane will understand . . . and through understanding, be joyfully aware of the happiness being given back to me.

The next few weeks remain a blur – but life carries on. Gradually, I begin to enjoy again the laughter of the village children and Dancing Stream becomes as my shadow, for she loves me most sincerely, just as I love her. Like her great-grandmother had said all those many years ago . . . she is happy with her life and others are happy to be around her. They feel contented with her relaxed and simple ways, for her life is uncomplicated and quite carefree. Her large eyes twinkle in the same way as my grandmother's had done and her gentle mannerisms often echo those of my greatest love. Just as her mother did, Dancing Stream also enjoys sitting with me by the falls, entranced by the colourful rainbows playing across the waters, as they cascade down. I notice how she will suddenly look up into the blue of the sky. Is it my Hawk she has seen? I feel that it is. Our son, Two Feathers, follows my own desires and he too comes to know of those wonderful healing energies and constantly works hard towards becoming our next Medicine Man. Sadly, many of our young people become restless, for their movements are curtailed and their sense of adventure taken away. They can no longer enjoy the Great Plains and the awe-inspiring features of Mother Earth. Their outlook is dulled and their learning spoiled. Life centres around this village where I was born and where one day my earth-body will fade.

My twin brother Two Shadows, continues to walk by my side, helping me to realise – there is still a lot for me to do. I still talk with the younger generation and try to uplift their spirits by taking them into the forest, or out along the riverbank. Hopefully, there they can enjoy doing the kind of things I had enjoyed doing as a boy . . . but the length of our journeys is always too short, the ground too familiar and the adventures too old. It is hard to fight against the loss they feel and openly show. It is not in their nature to stay at home. Where are our youth going to gain their experience of life in the wild, for there are no words to equal the actual sensation of being somewhere or becoming a part of something. It is quite impossible to convey to another the feeling of absolute freedom when riding across the open prairie or through the tall grasslands, or to sense how small we really are – and yet know we are a part of all we view. It is a feeling of complete oneness with both yourself and everything. To have the sky stretching above as far as the eye can see and to witness the herds of wild buffalo roaming across the Great Plains, quite oblivious to all but their own needs. To feel the earth tremble beneath your feet as they run past in their thousands, the dust-filled air swirling all around. To know the intensity of the stars in the night sky when you are completely alone. All these experiences touch your spirit deep within and let you become your true self . . . and in doing so, you learn. It is heart-breaking for me to think that all these sensations – our younger people will never really know, never really feel.

No matter how many times we are told about a certain thing, we still cannot grasp the full meaning of another's words until we happen to experience the doing of it for ourselves. When our close friends the Cheyenne rode into our village that early morning long ago and spoke to us of the Whiteman and the things they had seen, I sensed it was the beginning to the end of the freedom we knew and that our lives would change – but at the time though, I could not possibly realise just how very little would stay the same. Now I have experienced the different way of life we have been forced to lead . . . *now* I know. Experience is invaluable, yet although it is a great teacher it can also be a hard master. However, because of this, its lessons are usually never forgotten and they instil within us true wisdom, as well as knowledge. Unfortunately in this life, it is necessary to know of the bad, to appreciate the good. How can we enjoy the warmth of the campfire, if we have never felt the bitter cold of a hard winter and yet . . . when the child burns its fingers on the embers, it realises how fire can also hurt, if not handled in the right way. Yes, we need experience to fully learn.

A great amount of my time now, is spent in meditation, sending out healing thoughts for our people and the World. I also send out my thoughts for those who are completely lost when they return to the Spirit Realms, lost because of their hideous crimes on Earth. Not so much for the ones who are stumbling because of their ignorance, for they will be offered help from those of the Light. My thinking goes out to those who will have to first acknowledge what harm they've caused, both to others and to their own soul. They will have to face the consequences of their deeds. No-one will punish them, for they have indeed supplied their own punishment. What they have given to others – all the pain and the fear, will now be returned to them. They will dwell in those realms that house similar men. No pity is there, for these are people who have offered no pity to anyone, nor anything. What they have not given ... cannot be returned to them. It will be a long time before their souls become clean. This is the absolute fairness of Natural Law and this is how it is brought into play. I have not forgotten of course, those of my own kind who *did* retaliate against the atrocities levelled at our people by the Whites. Sadly, some of my brothers reacted with a great anger and hatred and I know this blemished their souls and that they too, will have had to make amends when they passed over. I know they will have been helped by healers, both from here and over there, to accept what they had done as also being wrong ... and so now I offer my healing thoughts for all who are trapped and suffering because of their own wrongful deeds. However, in no way do I condone any of their cruel behaviour.

I always wrap protection around myself whenever I think on these things. To those of the dark I say – reflect on what you have done and ask to be helped ... but your thinking must be sincere. If you genuinely wish to try and undo the harm you have caused, you must look for that speck of light which is always there, though you will not find it until you have experienced and witnessed in full, the pain you made others bear. Only then can you attempt to move ahead but remember, the hurt you gave to another, be it to animal or man, can be increased many times – for it will have also touched upon those whom they knew and loved. When sitting in meditation of any kind, it is important to know that you are in full control. Your spirit will be guided safely, if you walk in the Light. If you sense anything which you are not happy with, then you need to instantly dismiss it. Send it away. The more difficult thing to do is – once it has gone, do *not* start wondering what it was, for any continued thought on the subject will only invite it back. Once again surround yourself in love, light and truth. Everyone has freewill ... make sure you use yours, for while in meditation nobody can be governed by anyone else, only their own inner thoughts.

Through all of my travels along this pathway of life and indeed, through all the experiences I have embraced, I cannot lose faith with my Mother the Earth. She *is* our mother, no matter who we are – and she provides for our needs. I only wish the Whiteman would have a better understanding of this. I fear for those who have not been aware of their spiritual-self and have failed to listen to their conscience ... that wiser voice within. Everyone at some time in their earthly existence, has an opportunity to reach out and touch upon these gifts of the spirit, for as well as existing inside their own being, these gifts are all around them. Enlightenment may come at any time, through a simple thought or the merest glimpse, or it could be as a thunderous roar, but the chance to use our inner sense appears to us all. No one is left out. Unlike the lessons we need which, if not grasped, are given to us again and again, spiritual awareness is not something we have to pursue, for there are none so blind as those who do not wish to see and none so lost as those who never seek. All this I say in true humbleness and with a love that runs so deep. I too have made my mistakes. I too have uttered wrong words and had the wrong thoughts, but I know how previous errors can point out the right way and that learning is gained on the strangest of paths. However, I have and always will, hasten to retract any wrong I have done and try to make amends as soon as I can. Looking back on all I have known, I accept there will forever be . . . so much more to know. When we return to our Spirit Home, we will all continue to learn and hopefully, further progress. I truly believe hell is here on Earth and yet heaven can be here too, for again I would say to each and everyone – if we did not experience the bad, how would we come to recognise the good?

As I grow older the Elders of our village agree that my son can help me with my duties as Medicine Man. They know one day he will follow in my footsteps, for he possesses all the necessary caring qualities and healing gifts. I am, therefore, more free to just be of the earth and have time for myself. The forest becomes my retreat and I spend as much time there as in my own tipi. It has always called out to me . . . for I have always felt at home with the birds and the creatures living therein. I found long ago, I could easily relate to their way of life and since being a young child, I've had a great love for the trees. Thus it was destined to be – and thus it became.

"Just Reaching to the Light"

The time has come to say goodbye
. . . to journey on from here,
to meet again passed loved ones
who tenderly draw near,
look forward now with joyfulness,
reach for that Light ahead,
go forth into its brightness -
to where passed loved ones tread.

The time has come to leave behind
the worries and the strife,
which we encounter in this World
. . . that are a part of life,
take with you all our blessings,
the love which has been shown
and know we'll meet again one day -
when we too, travel home.

The time has come to let you go,
your spirit once more free,
no longer trapped inside a form
which could not let you be,
but free to soar in happiness
within those realms above,
where truth and peace and harmony
- surround you in great love.

13.8.98

"Just Different Kinds of Courage . . .
The Journey of Tasunke Witko"

Great Spirit of all I touch, see and hear,
in the silence I wait for you to draw near
and guide me on how to keep our Tribes clear
of the growing unrest, which covers this Sphere.

The pictures I'm shown in this Vision Quest
will give me the words to pass on to the rest
of those of our kind, suffering pain and distress
brought by the White-faces, who've now ventured West.

The break-up of our families threatens to start,
so I need to experience the love you impart
to keep myself balanced, having pledged in my heart . . .
I will fight this injustice which tears us apart.

On the Earth, in my body, I walk through this land,
yet I'm part of the valley, the mountain so grand,
the sparkling river, the plains and woodland -
I'm the leaf, I'm the moth, I'm the grain of red sand.

Thus my Spirit cries out for the freedom it's known
when our people first came and this place was our home,
to live on the prairie and with the beasts roam,
or stand in the quiet and spend time alone.

So it is that I sit here, upon a small mound,
amongst the wild creatures which may be around,
to blend with Mother Nature, through the harmony found
and breathe in your presence, each sight and each sound.

For the gift of true healing and the glow of your light
is as real as the fireflies which flash in the night,
the pure joy of the Snow Goose on her homeward flight
and the strength of the Buffalo's power and might.

Courage can come in many a way,
for many a reason, through many affray,
yet the courage which brings the unknown into play
- is the desire to ease another's dismay.

I ask for the courage for my people's sake,
to go to the white Fort, though it feels a mistake
and once there, with composure, the right actions make
in renewing the Peace, since all Treaties they break.

I ask for the courage to try and accept
the trial of our Nations, the challenges set,
the unfairness we face in attempts to connect
with a changing new world, which we sadly regret.

I ask for the courage to know in my mind
that our tribal ways may be lost to our kind
and the road which we follow, no more will we find,
as the life we all love, is left far behind.

I ask for the courage to try not to hate
those who abuse us, who do not relate
to the creatures and plant life, but only create
what they wish for themselves, ignoring our fate.

I ask for the courage for truth to be sought,
then the prayers of our Elders will not be for nought,
yet deep in my being, there lingers the thought –
a Spider's Web will be spun in this Fort.

Great Spirit of all I touch, hear and see,
with courage I go now to put forth my plea
in an effort to help my people stay free . . .
but I sense that tomorrow, they'll walk without me.

15.1.12

(*Tasunke Witko or 'Crazy Horse' was killed in cold blood
at Fort Robinson, Nebraska in 1877*)

CHAPTER FOURTEEN

I am

There is a sadness now that dwells in me. Not for myself, for soon I will be gone, but for others of my kind who must live on ... and for the lives of those who have yet to come. Life here is changing and I fear it is the end of the ways we have known. I do not fear those changes which will soon be happening to me, for I have never been afraid of 'death'. To me, death is simply the leaving behind of my physical body, which is only a covering wrapped around my spirit while it lives in this world. My spirit is the 'real' me. Although my state of being may change, my spirit will never die, for it is a part of the Great Spirit. When my body starts to fade and can no longer work, then my spirit will be released from its earthly frame – it will once again spend time in those Spirit Spheres. I know we all come from Spirit and to Spirit we will return, hopefully carrying within the knowledge which we came to Earth to gain, knowledge that only the Earthplane can give. As we travel from one existence to another, we become more and more aware of how there are so many different experiences needed, to enrich our soul.

When I move out of my body and pass from this world, I am truly lost to no-one. I can live on in the memories of those whom I love and who have loved me, until they make their journey home and we are all united once again. My loved ones who have already travelled forward from this life, will be there to welcome me. What is there to fear? 'Death' my friend, leads us onwards to that next phase of life within another dimension. It is a change from the slow vibrations of the Earth to the faster ones of the Spirit Realms. When born, we are separated from our mother by the cutting of the umbilical cord. When we return to Spirit, something similar will occur, for on our departure from this life, our spirit will be released from the body by the severance of the silver cord. This is a continuous stream of energy, attaching our spirit to our physical frame. It allows us to move in and out of our body while living here on the Earth, something which usually happens during a time of sleep or when in deep meditation. On the actual demise of the physical being, this cord will be detached and then the spirit will no longer be able to easily return, for it will have moved on into the Spirit Land. This is so, not just with ourselves, but with all living things.

Do not forget, our spiritual home in that world beyond is as real and as solid to us, as is our home here, yet in fact, nothing is solid . . . as the learned ones in both worlds know. Your own people have learnt that each and everything pulsates at a varying pace and on different vibrations. However, because our vibrations match those of the sphere in which we live, we relate to it and everything in it, as being solid. There are, though, certain ones who have learnt how to quicken their own vibration, to meet with those from Spirit who have managed to slow theirs down. I would say to you again – we must remember how we are all spirit, no matter where we may be and because of this, we can always communicate with each other. It is a matter of learning to use the right thoughts within our mind, for thoughts are indeed a powerful living energy in which all can blend and whether they be the thoughts of a man or of a creature, through them . . . all can relate and all can respond. The Indian knows this well and communes with our brothers and sisters in the animal kingdom. We speak to them in our meditations and

Vision Quests and we know if we listen with open minds, they will reply. We are all as relatives – for we are all children of the Great Spirit.

When the silver cord is broken and we are free of our earthly body, then our vibration is gradually quickened as we merge deeper into the Spirit Land. We become just as 'real' there as we appeared to be here, in this world. Sometimes, when a person has recently passed over, others have seen fleeting glimpses of them back on Earth. This is because their vibration is still heavy, hence it is easy for them to move in and out of the Earth's frequency. Their spirit is not yet fully attuned to the finer frequencies of its new home, but eventually it will be. Then they will find it much harder to show themselves in a different sphere. People ask . . . "Where can the Spirit World be found?" I fear they are looking too deeply for the answers they seek. The truth is never complicated; it is always quite simple. Different dimensions exist, but they do not take up space as we on Earth understand space to be. These dimensions are all around, each on a frequency of their own, for this is an ordinary part of the nature of things – it is just the way it is. Occasionally, these dimensions can intertwine and this is when something 'extra' ordinary is seen. Perhaps, when all can accept how they are a spirit-being, inhabiting an earthly body in this world they call home, then life will be far less complicated, for there will be a better understanding of the bond each one of us shares. This in turn will bring peace and love . . . and harmony will flow again. How very sad it is for my own people, the North American Indian, that this is not so at this moment in time. It seems the Whiteman does not want to understand our different customs and beliefs – and people tend to fear what they do not understand. Fear can cause aggression, which can quickly turn to violence . . . and then there is hurt.

I now feel a restlessness inside me, a desire to once more become a part of the wild places which I dearly love. I decide to venture out onto the Great Plains, even though my body is no longer as strong nor as quick as it once used to be. I know I must not forget how the Whiteman is all around and that he brings trouble to those of my kind. Quietly making my way down to the river where my pony is grazing, I pull myself up onto his sturdy back and suddenly, I feel young once again. Memories of sunny, carefree days come flooding into my mind and though my body still feels heavy, my heart is light. I am certain I can hear the distant laughter and boyish chatter of my friends with whom I would ride, so many years ago . . . Green Shoots, Red Flame, Lone Dog and of course, Blazing Bow, to name but a few. I make my way through the sparkling stream and across the river, heading towards the grasslands and open plains which lie spread out before me. Fortunately, my family appear to be busy elsewhere, for although nothing would have been said, I know they would have felt some concern at my riding alone. Gently, I urge my pony to quicken his pace. How good this feels. I am no longer an old man but the youth I once was. The tall green grasses are, as always, swaying from side to side and look *so* alive. The mountains appear to be just as high, with their snow-covered peaks bathed in the sun's rays. Mother Nature still unfolds her warmth over one and all. Far across the prairie I ride, my worries gone as I blend with the land, the rocks and the stones. Eventually my horse slows to a stop and we pause for a moment, while he enjoys the taste of new grass. I sit quite contentedly on his back, so happy to again be a part of this beautiful scene. It has been a long, long time since I felt so relaxed.

In the distance I see the shape of a bird, its feathers outlined against the blue sky. It seems far away and yet as I watch, its silhouette gradually becomes more clear. It is a hawk – and for a moment my reasoning departs and I wonder if it is he! My mind goes back in time and waving to him wildly, my soul fills with glee. As it circles around and flies in low over my head, tiny white specks become noticeable underneath one wing. I realise I have seen these markings before. This is one of his offspring and not even a male! Although I frown, I have to smile to myself, thinking how easily I was taken in. Truly – it must be old age! Even my pony gives a snort! Gathering together my excited thoughts, I carry on watching as she continues to glide skilfully along, the tips of her wings skimming the ground. Suddenly, I become fully aware that there is not one shadow but two, moving over the grass directly beneath where she flies. Are my eyes deceiving me again? I hesitate, not wanting to let my thoughts run amok. Whilst pondering this, one of the shadows stops and then slowly disappears . . . yet she and the remaining shadow continue flying on. Before believing what my eyes have just seen, I quickly note the position of the sun. Could this be a trick of the light? I know it is not! This time I smile broadly – knowing I am not wrong. My Hawk is letting me know he is near. How could I possibly leave him behind as I traverse these wide open spaces, just like we had both done together, so often in the past.

Pulling gently on the reins of my steed I urge him forward and into a trot. Lowering my head, we quickly gather speed, to ride at full stretch across the dry, red earth. Oh how my heart sings. What distant memories race through my mind. How good it is to recollect those great times of my youth and the freedom I had. The wind whistles past my ears and over my shoulders and my hair flies free like my pony's mane. Sadly, all too soon, it is time to stop. Both of us are breathing far too fast. The breeze blows cooler around my legs and a little shudder runs down my back. The day is drawing to a close, for the sun is descending in the now crimson sky. It has certainly uplifted me to be out on the

Great Plains – but it is time to turn my pony around and begin the ride home. First, I thank Wakan Tanka, for the strength my body has found to ride out here, thus giving me the chance to become a part of my homeland again. I also thank my Hawk. His presence makes me feel complete . . . yet it is becoming more and more evident how times are changing. Our young are now losing the kind of life we used to lead. Their gentleness is slowly fading with the ever increasing horrors they are coming to know. Nothing seems right with the world anymore. Life is not lived as it should be. I have grown old and do not wish to dwell in these changes I see. Life is precious and in the past, was so full and so free. We lived at one with the land and the different animals and birds. Our love spread out to all. The rivers, the forest, the grasslands and prairie, the canyons and majestic mountains. All were revered.

The Earth is our Mother, whose beautiful gifts lie all around for those who open their hearts and truly want to see. However, the world has moved forward and many great steps have been taken. Man has advanced – but where is his wisdom, his wisdom of self, his understanding of spirit and spiritual things? He seems to have lost these natural gifts. They lie hidden deep in his soul but they are there to be used and should be nurtured well. Yet his fine cities stand empty of Mother Earth's beauty, the many colours of Nature are lost to his eyes. His buildings rise higher and higher, shutting out the fresh clean air and his rivers seem unreal as they run their straight lines. The smell of the wild does not even exist and the hard concrete offers no comfort and upliftment of mind. His Spirit seems enclosed in a dismal abyss. Where are the flowers, the trees and the birds and where are the creatures who once wandered free? My tears flow greatly for these things gone amiss. Where is his love for his natural abode . . . the meadows and woodlands, valleys and hills, with the rain and the sunshine, the moon and the stars. Where is his oneness with our Mother the Earth? Where are his feelings of his own worth? Does he notice the sunrise, feel the wind and the breeze, sense the energies flow in the air all around, or is he oblivious to these natural joys which are there, to be found?

I embrace this far-reaching land with its immeasurable space and with Nature's own colours painted around, for I love the many varied shades of green in the forests and woods and across the grasslands and valleys, together with the different smells of the creatures who may roam through them, mingling with the scent from the trees. I love the blue of the winding rivers with their cool waters and the refreshment they bring, helping to sustain life. I love the orange and red of the prairie and the bright yellow sun high in the sky and the silver moon and sparkling stars in the blackness of night. I love the touch of the breeze and the sweet gentle rain. I love the open plains which seem to continue forever...and the sheer ruggedness of the mountain peaks with their shadows and deep gullies. I love all the wildlife – the beasts of the land, the birds of the air and the fish swimming in the streams. I love the ever-changing seasons of Mother Nature and I love the Great Spirit who is always there. He is all these things that I see, smell and hear and I am a part of them...and of him.

Riding slowly along, I now reach the familiar curve in the river known as Long Grass Creek and am suddenly overcome by an unbelievable feeling of love and of peace. I think about Running Water and raising my head, watch the late afternoon sky open up into beautiful shades of purple, lilac and blue. My body feels so light as I dismount from my pony. I kneel upon the soft earth which is still warm from the rays of the sun – this red earth upon which our village has stood for many years and upon which, as a boy I would lie looking up at the clouds floating across, high above. I can see fine wisps of smoke rising from our tipis and in the far distance I hear the sound of a drum. It reminds me of another time, another place, when I sat with my beloved Running Water so long ago. Through the softly fading light, beneath the green trees of the forest we both love, I am certain I see her walking slowly into view – and I feel the strong presence of my twin brother Two Shadows. I am also aware of my great friend, the Hawk. Yet again, I can hear the beating of his wings over my head. This time, I know they have come to guide my spirit safely home and as I go, I softly call out … "I am of the creatures and of the land – for I am Two Wings, a North American Lakota Indian."

>>>> <<<<

"Just Beneath Open Skies"

Out on the Great Plains I'm oblivious to all
… except the blue sky and the Eagle's lone call,
with the breeze in my hair and the grass 'neath my feet,
the aroma of sage makes the moment complete.

The strong rays of the sun beat down on my skin,
its energy touching my spirit within,
I lower my head and my eyes open wide
as I reach for my pony who stands by my side.

Although we are old both still can enjoy
the true freedom we found, when I rode as a boy
through canyons so deep and valleys so grand,
with the sound of swift hooves moving over the land.

Pronghorns would scatter, the elk turn and stare,
large moose would ignore us, just like the great bear,
coyote would bark, the prairie dogs run,
while the howl of the wolf meant night-time had come.

The passing of years is the blink of an eye . . .
the snowflake that melts, the storm passing by,
a sparkling raindrop, the falling of leaves,
a flickering shadow, the wind through the trees.

Across the prairie I do love to roam,
here in this great wilderness, I know as home
- and when the time comes for my spirit to leave,
I'll still have these adventures, so please do not grieve.

I will join with my Ancestors who've journeyed ahead,
this fact is for certain . . . yes, no-one is 'dead',
that flame once ignited, although it may dim,
can never be gone - for it lives deep within.

15.3.13

"Just a Meeting of Friends"

Once again I have drawn near,
to spend time within your sphere,
feel my presence ease the strain,
I am with you . . . speak my name.

I bring greetings from my world,
as past memories are unfurled,
let your inner-self recline
as we cross that bridge of time.

We are brothers, this you know,
bound together long ago
and the love which we knew then,
helps me join with you again.

Set your mind to wander free,
reaching out to welcome me,
find that space where peace and light
allow our souls to re-unite.

Bathed in truth you now will find,
precious moments can unwind,
as the spirit part of thee
dissolves into the harmony.

See the campfire burning low,
sit with others in its glow,
catch the scent of spruce and pine,
glimpse the moon and stars that shine.

My friend . . . I am now aware,
of whose company I share,
as far-off places I once knew
slowly come into my view.

Trees and grasslands, rivers wide,
open up on either side,
canyons, buffalo and deer,
in my consciousness appear.

An eagle swoops across the scene
and I know this is no dream,
for there below on open plain,
the piebald pony runs again.

This is my home from days gone by,
when I lived 'neath yonder sky
and roamed this pathway with my friend,
in whose presence I now blend.

For it is his loving power,
wrapped around me in this hour,
that enables me to be
amongst my Spirit family.

We move into the tipi grand,
where sit the Elders of our land,
I note their wisdom, humbly shown
and know . . . I never walk alone.

14.4.01

187

"Just Knowing the Spirit Within"

I am the Spirit within.

I am that part of you which lives forever,
at the moment encased in the form
which is known as you . . .
I am the part nobody can view.

I am the light that flickers therein,
that beam of light which forever shines,
sometimes dimly but always there . . .
the light which everything can share.

I am that spark of energy which is in all,
the energy which flows through all
and yet belongs to none . . .
I am the spark that cannot be gone.

I am the part of you that can touch the stars
and tread the ocean, feel the silence
and speak the thought . . .
without me, all is nought.

I am the Spirit within.

6.1.97

Other Books by the same Author:

the "Just Poems" books
including
Just Stories and Fairy Tales

Future Books:

"Butterfly Days"
Short Stories, Tales and Memories in Verse

>> <<

"Russell, Rae and Rusty"
The Story of a Young Boy and his Friends

>> <<

"Words from Beyond the Whispering Tree"
Short Stories in Verse relating to
the North American Indian

>> <<

Lightning Source UK Ltd.
Milton Keynes UK
UKOW04f0949211215

265130UK00001B/37/P